SALLY EMERSON is the award-winning author of novels including *Heat*, *Separation* and *Second Sight* and an anthologist of poetry and prose. She lives in London. Her website is www.sallyemerson.com.

PRAISE FOR

FIRE CHILD

'A taut, beautifully-constructed story moving simply but inexorably towards its cataclysmic ending'

Sunday Times

'A book that can be read as a comedy of modern manners, a love story or murder mystery – a rare achievement'

Literary Review

'With the narrative grip of Stephen King, Emerson's skill is in charging this novel with compulsiveness and foreboding'

Independent

'Told with power and skill. Sally Emerson has a talent for terror of the best kind, she understands obsession and hints chillingly at evil'

Daily Telegraph

'Sally Emerson writes like a dangerous angel'

Douglas Adams

'An ambitious exploration of morality in an irreligious society which explores evil in its modern forms. Adultery and sexual promiscuity dominate the narrative, which is set one autumn in contemporary London and told largely through the diaries of the two protagonists, the irresistibly sensual Tessa Armstrong and her diabolical arsonist love, Martin Sherman, who appears at first to be a contemporary Dr Faustus.

At 13, Tessa artfully combines the well-honed skills of an accomplished courtesan with contrived innocence. Unaffected by her lovers' distress, she tosses them off like clothes. But when her father's death, for which she feels responsible, pierces Tessa's callous exterior, seduction stops being fun. Frightened by her own power over men, Tessa is suddenly troubled by a conscience she never realized she had.

Emerson has provided us with a thought-provoking, enigmatic novel, which raises questions that reach far beyond the confines of its plot'

Washington Post

'The two protagonists are like sticks of dynamite blazing a trail which glimmers and crackles… The clever use of their respective diaries, which span only a month and a day, effectively presents a wealth of detail, while moving the story swiftly forward'

Sunday Times

'A several-layered novel about a woman who from the age of 12 seduces and destroys men. A spare, subtle story of lust, love, violence and comedy'

Susan Crosland

ALSO BY SALLY EMERSON

Heat

Separation

Second Sight

Listeners

Broken Bodies

FIRE CHILD

SALLY EMERSON

QUARTET BOOKS

First published in Great Britain by Michael Joseph Ltd in 1987
Published by Quartet Books in 2017
A member of the Namara Group
27 Goodge Street, London, W1T 2LD

A catalogue record for this book is available from the British Library

ISBN 9780704374287

Typeset by Tetragon, London
Printed and bound in Great Britain by TJ International Ltd, Padstow, Cornwall

To my dear mother, Ceris Emerson

Some say the world will end in fire,
Some say in ice.
From what I've tasted of desire
I hold with those who favour fire.

ROBERT FROST

PART I

Martin Sherman

Baalbec Road, Highbury, N5
Friday 1 September

I HAVE GINGERY HAIR AND NO MONEY, AND BAD HABITS LIKE eating cold baked beans out of the tin. My small room is heated by a two-bar electric fire, which I keep on most of the time. My landlady thinks the world of me. This is actually not a great compliment as my landlady is stupid and has the hips of a hippopotamus. Her breasts are nearly as large. They sway from side to side. Sometimes when she wobbles down the stairs quickly I fear she's going to lose one. I am twenty years old. She's well over fifty.

She charges me less than the others.

The others are an odd lot too. There's Mr Phillips who looks like a praying mantis, and indeed has religious proclivities, or so my landlady tells me. He hardly ever speaks to anyone. He looms around the bathroom occasionally, but that appears to be very nearly his only social contact.

His room contains just a bed, a small kitchen table, one chair, one armchair, a few books and an old cooker. Mind you, my room is not much livelier.

A student couple live in a room on the top floor. Both have an imaginative array of acne. Their faces are never dull. Each new day brings a fresh spot, or a fresh development to an existing one. Jerry and Mary are always by each other's side. Sometimes I wonder if they are in fact joined: Siamese twins masquerading as a loving couple. They play pop music very loudly and seem particularly to enjoy scratched records.

My parents are very concerned about my early retirement to this quiet spot with its sloping floor, its dishcloth curtains, its faint smell of mummified rat. They expected a great deal more of me.

Some of the rooms in the house are so damp and dilapidated that they're uninhabitable. It's a shame really. The landlady lived here with her family as a child, and inherited it when her parents died. Now she lives in one ground-floor room with a kitchen extension which is about to collapse. Whenever it rains, the kitchen fittings become islands on a lake. Her husband died years ago and Mrs Monson (that's the old girl's name) simply cannot cope, in spite of her part-time job in a dress factory. The student couple are always late with their rent. She shakes her head sadly. They apologize in unison like Tweedledum and Tweedledee. Next week, the same thing happens. Apparently they're both studying catering at a college in Finsbury. Mrs Monson seems faintly proud of having 'students' in her house. She's rather more doubtful about Mr Phillips, although he pays up promptly. His eyes swerve nervously when asked about his job, which I gather is something to do with debt collecting. Presumably he works behind a desk, perhaps just composing threatening letters. I can't imagine his being sent to rough anyone up. Unless he's paid just to appear at people's windows to frighten them with his gaunt face and huge bony hands.

Mrs Monson should sell Hope Villa (the name in the stained-glass panel above the door). It's a Victorian monster, situated near the station and overlooking Highbury Fields, a kind of village green, at the back. It's only a short distance from the centre of London.

All the other houses in the terrace have been renovated and moved into by nice, middle-class families, like so much of this area of north London. There is restoration going on in every street: old wallpaper ripped off, gas fires flung out, new cornices plastered in.

This place is too big for her to manage, and it would fetch a very good price.

The only problem is that it would be difficult to get rid of tenants like myself.

In the supermarket I just stamp and stack tins. It is not a high-powered job. The supermarket employees drift in and out just like the customers. Nobody seems to stay for more than a few weeks. I've been hiding there for five years. My parents, who are middle class, disapprove of my job, saying that it's not worthwhile. Of course it's not worthwhile. However, it is peaceful and undemanding. I especially enjoy messing about with the tins, building them into tower blocks of squares or pyramids. And there is usually some absurd new product to amuse me – tinned curry, calorie-free jam, instant risotto.

The customers can be tiresome. Once a mild-looking middle-aged woman hit me over the head with her umbrella, then burst into tears; all because I'd said the milk was back down the aisle where she'd come from.

I spend much of my free time reading science fiction and books on astronomy. Although I like to think about the end of things – the universe disappearing, earth burning up, galaxies hurtling away from each other – such thoughts scare me. But I have felt safe in the supermarket and up in my overheated little room. The minutes and the hours have melted not disagreeably into days; I even sometimes thought that I might have got through my life without too much bother.

Occasionally, in the evenings, I found myself putting on a suit and going out and looking for her in clubs and bars. But I didn't really want to find her.

I wanted to dedicate myself to a solitary life of no achievement, like Mr Phillips, at fifty alone in one room with only a few books and an old cooker. I knew what the alternative would be for me, or knew something of what it would be. And hiding from it seemed like the best bet.

But of course I have been lonely. Although I have had girl-friends none of them has been her. And although I had – until now – turned my back on ambition, I was still subject to occasional severe attacks of that particular brand of panic which I suspect makes people ambitious (chopping off enemies heads probably allayed the panic of Genghis Khan, writing plays no doubt helped Shakespeare's).

But then I had that dream. I dreamt I met the devil standing under a lamppost at night, in the rain. With raincoat collar turned up and trilby turned down, he looked like a crook from an old black-and-white movie. And yet, as is the way of dreams, I knew who he really was without his having to admit it.

Of course I have seen him before, in different forms. I have seen him as the charming Mephistopheles of *Faustus*. I have seen him swinging his umbrella in inventive old films. I have seen him by my bed at night as a child. I have seen him in the mirror.

Yet somehow I thought he wouldn't find me here, in my hide-out. I just wanted to dawdle away my life. Do nothing. Contribute nothing. Leave it exactly as I found it. And then he comes with his smiles and his sneers.

2

TESSA ARMSTRONG

Northwood Road, Highbury, N5
Friday 1 September

I AM VERY THIN AND FIND IT HARD TO EAT. SOMETIMES I think I'm starving myself to death because I'm tired of existing. I don't like myself. Ever since I killed my father I have lost hope. That was five years ago. I was just fifteen.

Before that my only problem in life was to decide whether to be an actress, a journalist like my father, or a chat show hostess. But at the same time, I realize now, I was cold. The drawer of this desk where I sit is full of love letters. I used to read them out to my girlfriends at school, in particular to my best friend Nicola, who was prettier than the other girls and wickeder. They were children, while Nicola and I were born old. She was the daughter of a politician. I haven't seen her for five years but we fell out long before that, one evening; an evening which caused quite a scandal.

I still like to read my old letters.

I think I was made with a very large Tessa-shaped hole in my mind and heart. I also think I was very brave to manage without you all those years. I loved you so instantly, and it's the same love I feel now, much stronger and deeper now, and growing so much all the time, but it's the same love. It's hard to see how it arrived like that, just suddenly and fully formed and without a moment's hesitation or doubt. You were the one, you are the one, you always will be the one. Darling, if I didn't know from experience that I will be more in love with you tomorrow than I am today and will be more in love with you still next week, I would say that I love you absolutely.

That one was written by a photographer I met in a park. He left the country when I grew bored and refused to see him. Even at the time my ability to inspire intense love rather surprised me. Especially as the love was always unreciprocated.

In those days, when my father was alive, we had a house in south London full of windows – bay windows, round windows, French windows – next door to three young boys and their parents. When the eldest boy Philip was thirteen, he started to want to swap stamps with me. Before that, I had been good only as a snowball target. I caught him staring at me intently as I examined his lovely Chinese stamps covered in dragons and sputniks on the floor of my bedroom. I suggested he give them all to me in exchange for just one dull brown Norwegian stamp featuring a man with a small beard. He agreed, and for the first time I recognized my power. I remember the faint dark hairs above his lips and the furtive way he looked at me.

He never tried to touch me. Occasionally my arm would brush his, as if in error, and he would blush. He had big ears, short hair and an excellent stamp collection – until it was decimated by my unfair offers.

One day during an endless hot summer holiday I called round to swap stamps with Philip wearing a pretty backless dress, hoping to get better stamps that way. But Philip was out, playing cricket. His two brothers and mother were out too.

His handsome father, however, was in.

He had been mowing the lawn in his shorts, and had sweat on his face and a beer in his hand. He invited me in for a Coca-Cola.

8

'Your lawn looks very nice, Mr Brown,' I said as I stood at the window of the breakfast room.

I felt his hands on my bare arms.

'Yes it does, doesn't it?' he said in an ordinary voice as though nothing out of the ordinary were happening. His hands on my arms gave me an agreeable sensation, somewhere between a shiver and a burn. He kissed the hot nape of my neck.

'Where's my Coca-Cola, Mr Brown?' I asked softly.

He stopped kissing to reply: 'It's on the table behind you. Do you want a glass or a straw?'

'No thank you very much. I'll drink it from the can… in a minute.'

His hands were round my waist – big, tough, man's hands. I liked the smell of his sweat. His hands moved upwards and pushed my breasts up. I closed my eyes in pleasure as Mr Brown kissed the back of my head and murmured into my hair. He turned me round and put his lips on mine.

It was not the first time I had been kissed but it was easily the best. The kisses of boys were inept: a slobbery blurring of lips.

Mr Brown gave complicated kisses. His tongue became one second like a small fish let loose in my mouth – it darted delightfully all over the place. The next second his tongue changed into a warm snake thrusting and pushing.

I stood limply and gave myself up to the pleasure.

His hand was undoing the buttons of my dress when the phone rang in the next room.

He started.

'Don't answer,' I said.

He looked down at me with a dazed expression, as though he didn't know who I was or how I'd got there.

'Don't answer it,' I repeated firmly.

His forehead puckered.

9

'Don't frown at me like that,' I said. 'You don't look quite so handsome when you frown.'

He continued to stare at me.

The phone seemed to be ringing louder and louder into the silence.

'Tessa, tell me. How old are you?'

'Nearly thirteen,' I replied, with a hint of pride. I was fed up with being twelve and being treated like a child.

He took a step back, then swung away, out of the room.

A minute or two later he returned. His eyes were piercing and blue and sort of scared.

'That was the boys saying they'll be back soon.'

I crossed my arms. 'I haven't had my Coca-Cola yet.'

He handed me the can. I watched him as I drank. A little dribbled down my chin. I wiped it off with the back of my hand.

His face was flushed.

He looked past me, through the window, at his garden with its tree house and its swings.

'They'll be back soon,' he repeated.

I put my arms around him, and looked up, big-eyed, sweet, very young.

His lips returned to mine.

We made love a few minutes later on the floor, before the boys returned home. It was my first time. I quite enjoyed it.

Afterwards, he dressed quickly and would not meet my eyes.

For the next few weekends I watched his house from my parents' bedroom and when I was sure he was alone I'd call round asking for Philip. Always Philip's father offered me Coca-Cola. Always he tried not to make love to me. Always he did make love to me, and always he dressed quickly afterwards and would not meet my eyes.

During those weeks he lost a lot of weight and by the end was rather haggard and not as attractive as at first, so I became less interested.

I told him on the phone that I was going back to school and, what with homework and friends, would not have time to mess about with him any more. He went very quiet.

'Let's think of it as a holiday romance,' I said.

He wrote me letters and hung around to see me after school (I told everyone he was my uncle because by now he didn't look at all good).

One day the letters stopped and soon afterwards there was a 'For Sale' notice outside the Browns' house.

My father told me that poor Mr Brown had had some kind of breakdown and that he and his family were moving to the country once he was out of hospital.

It was the first time I had reason to be scared of myself.

Now I have less reason to be scared of myself. I could surely not be a threat to any man. My hair has gone grey. At twenty I have given up everything. I hardly eat. I don't read. I never go out, except to work. I have not bought any clothes for years, living in the shadows here.

3

MARTIN SHERMAN

Saturday 2 September

IN ISLINGTON THERE ARE LEAVES EVERYWHERE – IN THE gutters, on the pavements, carried by the wind which in the last few days has come to stir up the streets; dying leaves lie on the ground, their veins threaded with black. Autumn has come early this year.

In my dreams the girl I'm looking for asks me to climb down the rope of her hair into hell.

Even this diary, or whatever it is, has got damp from a leak in the window. Its lined pages curl up at the edges like the lino in the bathroom which stops the door from closing properly.

On the way to work people hurry along with their heads down and umbrellas up, darting through the shadows as if on some secret mission, barging others out of their way, covering their faces.

Last night as I tried to sleep I ran through in my mind every detail of this house, Hope Villa, as though it were no longer there. I recalled its every frayed carpet, every bit of peeling wallpaper, every dusty corner, every curve of staircase, with affection, as though it had already gone, as though it had already burnt down.

I suppose I have always been interested in fire.

My uncle was the first to observe my interest.

It was partly his fault. He first told me about the moment that the universe exploded from a single piece of matter, a giant primeval atom concentrated at a single point in space. I saw a vast explosion of fire which destroyed everything to create everything. This was all somehow related, in my child's mind, to my uncle's red beard, which I had observed was made up of many bits, like a fire.

He and I get on well most of the time. He is my godfather and always took a great interest in me and my education. He is unmarried. And although he has girlfriends, he appears curiously uninterested in them. I rather suspect he might be gay, except that the girls would tend to disprove this and I have no evidence apart from his obsession with paintings and his black sheets and one leather coat.

He's a wealthy stockbroker but his main interest is collecting early twentieth-century watercolours, chiefly it seems ones of bad weather which no doubt suit his somewhat depressive nature.

Like everyone else, he much prefers me to my older brother, a dreary person who tries desperately hard to do well and yet somehow always seems to fail. My brother is now an embittered second-rate lawyer, bewildered as to why he should still envy me, a stacker in a supermarket. He has a wife I seduced one Christmas and a child. They both seem rather to despise my brother although he works hard and makes the most of his small talents.

Once when I was about six I was round at my uncle's. He was writing letters in his library while I played in the garden on the bicycle he had bought me. His head was down. He wasn't watching me. I wandered down into the shed by the billiard room.

There were faint cobwebs over the dusty windows, an old rug on the floor (he had organized it as my own little house), a few lost winter leaves lying in the corners and, on a small shelf, some rusty nails and a box of matches.

My initial desire was merely to light the matches.

In our main room at home we had a coal fire, and my father often made bonfires in the garden. When he stood by the flames his face lit up and was transformed from the likeably dull one which went quietly about his affairs to something red and exultant.

It occurred to me that the wooden shed would look very pretty in flames.

It took a little time to organize the fire.

I wandered back into the house, found a few old newspapers in the cupboard under the stairs, and returned with them to the shed.

My uncle looked up once from his letters and smiled vaguely, presumably at my air of busyness (I was a pretty child, with curly red hair, freckles and innocent blue eyes).

The next trip was to the garage.

Of course the paraffin wasn't an absolute necessity, but I thought it would make the fire more dramatic. Besides, I wanted the excitement of finding the can of paraffin, and pouring it, without being seen. I didn't like things to be too easy. Because I was bright, everything was usually too easy for me.

With a quick glance to make sure my uncle was not watching, I lugged the can out of the garage along the outskirts of the garden, by the hedges, around the back of the billiard room, past the walnut tree, and to the shed, which stood a little way away from anything else.

My heart was beginning to beat fast.

It was quite dark, and very private here.

I tore up and rolled the newspapers into thin worms, as my father had shown me, and tossed them over the wooden floor of the shed before splashing paraffin over the newspaper, the rug, the floor and the walls. I laid the rest of the newspaper into a long black-and-white fuse.

I remember being vaguely concerned that my behaviour might get me into trouble, but then brushed that thought away because I had decided that the punishment, however bad, would not be as bad as the pleasure of seeing the shed burn would be good. Besides, I knew there was a chance that I would get away with it, as I was an accomplished liar.

I lit one match, then blew it out.

I lit another match, and blew that out.

A fly was caught in the spider's soft string by the window and I remember thinking of the shed as its funeral pyre.

I knelt down, struck a match, and as it dropped on to the touchpaper I stood well back.

The flames took a while to consume the building. As I watched through the window they ate slowly through the rug – I worried lest I had not applied enough paraffin – and then, like someone who suddenly realizes he is hungrier than he thought, the fire swallowed up the whole shed in a roar of delight.

My uncle came running down the garden.

'Stand back,' he shouted.

I stood a little further back.

He grabbed my arm and pulled me even further away.

I was, I recall, faintly surprised that he was more concerned about me than his shed.

He didn't try to put out the fire.

For a while he was as mesmerized as I was.

As the flames died down he said, 'What happened?' in an odd kind of voice.

'It was an accident,' I said, looking straight into his eyes. 'I was playing with the matches you left in the shed and I dropped one and the whole place caught fire. I'm terribly sorry, really I am.'

'I see,' he said.

I had my hands on my hips, and I was shaking my head sorrowfully, meaning to look like a man who sees his life's work gone.

But my face clearly expressed something else.

'Come on,' said my uncle, clamping my arm, 'and look at yourself in the mirror.'

He dragged me across the lawn, and up the stairs.

He took me into his bedroom and stood me in front of his long wardrobe mirror.

I blinked.

My face was radiant.

'You loved it, didn't you?' he said.

I nodded.

'You started it on purpose, didn't you?'

'Well…'

'I won't tell your mother. If you don't do it again. And if you tell me the truth, although I know that is against your principles. I know you, Martin. You are a liar and a wicked little wretch. You are also, as you know only too well, an adorable little child.'

He was crouching behind me, holding my arms.

I could see his big-jowled face at my left shoulder, watching me through the mirror.

His eyes were hooded, like my mother's, only they gave him an air of sleepy content whereas they gave my mother that of a hungry bird of prey.

That day, however, there was something a touch disturbing about his appearance. I could see he was angry with me but there was something else too, which I never saw again.

'I did enjoy it. But I didn't burn it down. Honestly,' I said. I had learnt that it was wiser to tell a bit of the truth if in trouble.

'You could have been killed.' He turned me round. 'You don't want to burn to death, do you?'

I shook my head.

'Well if you play with fire you will. One day. I know you don't care about other people, so I won't use that as a threat. But yourself. You care about yourself, don't you?'

I nodded.

'Well then.'

He smiled at me, and I felt a huge relief.

'I'd better take you home. And when you get home you'd better change your clothes immediately, but right now you'd better wash your hands, in the bathroom through there.'

He turned his back and left the room.

'You smell of paraffin,' he said, as he left.

It was a while before I began to experiment with flames again.

In those days we lived in a large red-brick Victorian house on the outskirts of Epsom, set well back from a wide, quite busy road which led up to Epsom Downs.

There was something deadly about the road, with its prosperous houses each set at exactly the same distance apart.

I had come to dislike the bleak Downs too, especially the empty Grandstand, staring out at the windswept slopes as if waiting for someone or something that would never come back.

It occurred to me that we should move.

At that time my mother was not as she is now, a tough left-wing politician. She concentrated on her house, her children, the community and a few of what she called her 'hobbies', learning Russian and studying law at evening classes. She is far cleverer than my father, although she has had no formal education.

Broad-shouldered and determined, she has always struck me as an unattractive parent. And I used to hate the way she would never leave me alone. She referred to herself as 'pottering' but she pottered about as much as a busy vulture. Even when I was tiny I can remember her swooping about the place, snatching up clothes from the floor, thrusting my brother and me into nursery school, whooshing down to make me draw a face properly as I sat at the miniature desk given to me one birthday to the envy of my brother. Later, she stood cheering and badly dressed at school sports days, read and admired my essays, studied my maths answers with respect. She was always pointing out how much I looked like her, which I don't, except that she had reddish hair. She even claimed my cleverness as her own – 'He takes after me' – as though she wished to gobble me all up.

The fire at our house was at least a positive creation, or anyway a creation.

Preparation for it diverted me for about a week, and its aftermath changed our lives.

It started one lunchtime (I had scurried home from school) and raged until late afternoon.

The police afterwards said it must have been started by a burglar or perhaps by an electrical fault. The inspector, a plump fellow, wandered round the charred ruins shaking his head.

I wanted to dance about the place like an imp. It was such a delightful change.

My mother's home-made curtains had gone, her excessively clean rooms, my old school exercise books with their grade As, our table-tennis table, all the paraphernalia of my goody-goody past.

Half a chair lay on what had been the kitchen floor, as though there had been a fight. Another chair had turned to charcoal.

The windows had all smashed and now we could see the garden properly through the skeleton window frames which remained.

My father was dazed as we wandered that evening through the ground floor which was smoking in places like a very old volcano.

'Why didn't someone notice earlier? It's incredible,' he said. 'The destruction.'

'Coincidence,' said the inspector, stepping over an exploded television set with its entrails out. 'No one happening to notice until too late. They must have all been busy elsewhere or looking in another direction.'

'All my medical books. All her recipe books. They've all gone,' said my father.

My mother was looking unusually calm, and taller and more relaxed than I'd seen her for a long time. She had a slight smile on her lips as she made her way through the debris.

I had of course spent the afternoon being busily conspicuous at school. My hand shot up at every question during the history period, which I recall was about Elizabeth I and her Parliaments, as most history lessons were.

I had walked slowly back from school that day, not wishing to be first to arrive. But when I saw the fire engines all over the road, I knew my planning had paid off and I ran towards the flames.

From a distance I had seen my mother watching the burning house tranquilly from the other side of the road, a chunky figure in a green raincoat, untidy hair, still clutching her shopping bag. Nobody would have known it was her house which was burning.

When I came up to her she just put her arm around my waist and we watched together.

'The odd thing is,' she said after a long time, 'I find I don't really mind at all.'

We stayed that night and the next three months at my uncle's, and from the day of the fire my mother changed. Perhaps it reminded her that she was mortal, or maybe it just released her from the past.

For a few days she was very thoughtful, and then she started doing things. While my father fretted, she made sure that we received an enormous insurance payout, and she looked for a new house – a functional modern house because she no longer believed in houses.

At first the removal of her attention seemed a great relief, but soon it left me a little desolate, as it did my father, a doctor, who took to driving off to play bridge with friends.

I can remember an evening early on at my uncle's. My uncle was out with one of his girlfriends (we only ever saw glimpses of these girls – through the window, in the hall, from a distance. They were blonde and well dressed, of various ages).

The four of us, my mother, father, my brother Henry and myself were all sitting like sullen sculptures over the beige expanse of the living room. There was a grey light coming through the picture windows and for a moment it seemed that we were all tainted by grey – my mother, glancing up at her brother's library, wanting so much more than she would ever achieve; my father in an armchair with tweedy jacket and pipe, a museum model of a family man; Henry watching my mother with worship in his eyes; and me, slouched on my chair, watching the sunlight show up in the dust in the air, not belonging to any particular time or place.

The next weekend my parents and brother went to see my father's father, who was very ill.

I asked to come too, as I did not wish to be left alone with my uncle, but they refused, saying that I was too young to see someone dying.

My uncle had been treating me oddly since we'd been staying with him, without his usual jollity and warmth.

'So,' he said soon after they had left, as we sat facing each other over a spread of hard-boiled eggs, tomatoes, lettuce and thick lumps of ham.

We were in his American-style kitchen, one on each side of the counter which jutted into the centre of the room. I was facing the garden, looking out through the wide picture window.

'You and I are alone now,' he said.

I nodded, and quickly crammed my mouth full of bread. My legs, with their short grey socks and lace-up shoes, dangled down from the high stool, not reaching the floor.

There is something I wish to talk to you about.'

I tried to fit a boiled egg into my mouth.

I nodded.

I liked my uncle, even though the way he was looking at me now was unpleasant. It was a brooding, serious look.

'Nobody else seems to be aware of what you are like,' he said. 'You simply cannot continue in this way.'

I kicked my legs against the counter and examined the lettuce leaf on my plate, not remorsefully but to give me time to gather my expressions.

He leaned forward and his big hand jerked my head back so that our blue eyes met.

I blinked at him, thinking it wise not to deny anything as he hadn't yet accused me of anything.

His black cat jumped on the table and rubbed against his arm. He let me go and caressed her slowly, gently. She purred and dipped her back in pleasure.

'I haven't said anything to your mother, though I suspect in her heart she knows. She's not a fool you know.'

I took a tomato and sank my teeth into it.

'Do you have friends, Martin?'

I nodded.

'That's what your mother said. And you do well at school?'

I nodded again.

'Are you unhappy?'

I shook my head.

'Everyone seems to like and admire you. God knows why, I'm at fault too. Charm, I suppose. But what I want to know is why you are as you are. Is it just youthful high spirits? Boredom? Something you'll grow out of? Or is it something more than that? Is it, Martin? Will you always be like this?'

I put my head to one side.

'I'm awfully sorry. I should like to help, but I have no idea what you're talking about,' I said, and smiled.

His eyes stopped for a moment, the way people's do when they're very angry, and he stepped down from his stool.

I was suddenly apprehensive.

He took me into his study, which he calls his 'library'.

His 'library' was his favourite room. It had a navy carpet while the fitted carpets elsewhere which oozed all over the floors were deep pile white. On the walls were some of his paintings – a few cupids hopping about with a pretty girl in one, a misty landscape like Epsom Downs on a dismal day in another, a third with a few streetlights and a wet street. He was proud of his collection of paintings, which he had built up carefully over the years, and had once told me they were worth a great deal of money and that he would leave them to me when he died.

As he beat me I stared at the carpet where bits of cotton spiralled like distant galaxies.

It was warm that day, and after he had beaten me we walked in the garden together.

We didn't speak as we walked.

His hands were shaking, and he no longer seemed strong and reliable.

We never discussed the episode, and I believe he thought he had cured me; which he sort of had, for a while.

We moved to the new house, a little modern place further away from Epsom Downs, and I didn't see my uncle much any more.

I spent most of the time in my room playing chess with myself and reading books. I read the Bible, enjoying Genesis most of all: 'In the beginning God created the heaven and the earth. And the earth was without form, and void; and darkness was upon the face of the deep.'

I read other books too, and was particularly interested in one which tried to explain why, during the history of the earth, whole species have died out.

But on the whole I cared about very little. There seemed little point in anything.

After all, even the universe will eventually fold in on itself and nothing will be left but blackness. By that time earth will have long ceased to exist. Nothing will happen in this blackness. Time won't exist, or place. Any idea people have of immortalizing themselves through art or children or colonizing other planets is absurd. Even in the unlikely event of us not wiping ourselves out, we'll be wiped out because the whole thing will pack up. Caput. Curtains. I hope the devil does exist. At least he would be able to hear himself chortling in the blackness at his joke.

And sanctimonious geography teachers tried to make me learn about crops in Peru! They should have taught us instead what time is if it can cease to exist, and whether there are universes beyond the universe.

Instead they wasted our time.

The scripture lessons were equally footling – what Christ said to whom where and what his house looked like; whereas what I wanted to know was does the devil exist or not and is God supposed to be the boss of the whole caboodle including all the other universes that might be floating around millions and millions and millions of miles away, and are they all governed by the same moral laws, and if they cease to function will there still be morality drifting around unattached in infinite space? Was my amorality something purely at variance with the social laws of earth, or did it represent a deeper, more lasting, evil?

The only subjects which involved me at all at school were science and literature, in particular early literature in which people addressed themselves to problems which matter, such as the nature of hell (I liked Dante's *Inferno* and *Paradise Lost*).

Meanwhile my mother gained in vigour. She joined council committees and campaigned for social services while my father became a slighter and slighter person. He was always on the phone to patients or visiting patients, as though he only existed in his capacity as doctor.

Broad, striding, efficient, my mother began to remind me of a sturdy Russian worker. She even cropped her hair short, which before had been the one misfitting part of her, rather thick and wild and the wrong kind of length, loitering somewhere around her ears.

Her eyes which had always been steely became even colder.

Sometimes I saw exhilaration in her face, but few other emotions.

It was a relief to me when the time came when I could leave school and escape the atmosphere in that empty house.

My mother was outraged at my leaving school early ('A boy of your brains,' she protested, etc, as did all the teachers). My father did his best to make me stay.

But I wanted to be alone for a while.

And now I have been alone for a long time, and all that time I've been looking for her, and I am growing tired of being alone.

Sometimes it seems that I've spent not just this lifetime but other lifetimes searching for her, and once I find her I can be myself.

In clubs and pubs I have picked girls up, once or twice in the half-light mistaking them for her but having no interest in them once I knew who they were – ordinary, giggling girls who were nothing like her.

4

Tessa Armstrong

Saturday 2 September

THIS BEDROOM IS THE SAME AS IT WAS THE DAY MY MOTHER and I moved into the house a few months after my father's death: grey embossed wallpaper, thin satiny curtains, a cord carpet, and a close-up view of the house across the street. It seems to lean forward, over ours.

My mother, however, repainted her bedroom in a vulgar pink. She should have left it as it was when we first arrived, in mourning.

I've been in mourning for five years now. I've been cut off from everything, living in a dream, a kind of nightmare in which the memory of the day my father died plays in my mind over and over again. It was all the fault of the man who was my lover. Afterwards, he kept phoning me up but I refused ever to speak to him. I just put down the phone on him, and I returned his letters unopened. Once, before I put down the phone, he managed to tell me that he loved me. But I didn't want to know that. I had given up being loved by men. I had given everything up. I had even tried to give up hating my old lover, my father's best friend. I just passed through the hours of my life trying not to think, trying not to notice anything, trying not to be anyone.

Now, and I don't know quite why, I am beginning to notice things again. Perhaps my period of mourning is over. Perhaps it is this particular autumn that is making me come alive again. Already the leaves are changing colour and the sense of life and movement and death seep beneath my skin and make me look different.

Last night, after writing my diary, I found myself dressing up in a red satin dress I wore for a ball once, before my father died. My mother was out so I took her long black gloves from her drawer, and her jewellery. My hair and neck were covered in glittery false diamonds. I put on her make-up too; plenty of it, so that my eyes were silver, surrounded by black kohl, and my lips were scarlet.

I stood in front of her long mirror, and smiled.

I was so immersed in watching the creature in the mirror, with the hair full of diamonds, that I didn't hear my mother come home.

When she opened the door of her bedroom and saw me smiling, she gasped. Her skin lost its colour. She put her hand to her mouth.

'Tessa!' she said.

I turned.

'What's the matter?' I said. 'Where have you been?'

'Why I... you've never asked me that before.'

'I've never cared. I haven't been noticing much, have I?' I took a step closer to her, and she took a step back.

'You're wearing my jewellery,' she said. 'And my make-up.'

'But when I think back... where do you go most nights? You've got a boyfriend, haven't you?'

'And why shouldn't I?'

'You've just been out with him.'

'Perhaps I have.'

'You're being unfaithful to my father.'

'Your father's dead.'

'I made you promise you wouldn't have a boyfriend.'

'You were hysterical about it. I promised in order to keep you quiet. You've been severely disturbed, darling.'

'You still promised.'

'It's nothing... important.'

'Why haven't I met him? Why haven't you brought him back here?'

'I didn't think you'd want to meet him.'

I glanced at myself in the mirror, and my eyes glittered.

'He's been here though,' I said, 'while I've been out at work, hasn't he? Thinking back… I've felt that someone… has been here. He's been in my room, too, hasn't he?'

'Of course not. Now please leave my room.'

My mother and I have never been close, and we have never confided in each other. Other people's mothers took their children to lunchtime treats and shopping trips, but mine never did. I am not complaining about a deprived childhood: my father's devotion more than made up for my mother's distance. It is just that I don't think she ever liked me much, and I rather liked her because she was so beautiful.

Her room now looks like that of a teenager – perfume, creams, knickers, dresses, all over the place.

In my room, however, there are no pictures, no books, no rugs. Only my old desk, my chair and my bed remain from our other house. I thought that, like a person who knows she is dying and wants to leave nothing behind, I was slowly rubbing myself out, getting rid of my possessions and my personality and my life.

And yet this weekend, for the first time in five years, I find myself wanting to write things down in my diary. Perhaps it is because I am dying. Or perhaps I am coming back to life. I only cause pain. Perhaps I should tear up my old diaries and my old love letters. Perhaps I should forget what I was. But how can I? At least I have some memories. It is all I have. Surely I can be allowed some memories?

One lover in particular, Simon, wrote such good letters. I have one here – ten sides of it – written in careful black handwriting on thick yellow paper. It is torn in one corner after being trapped – along with a pressed rose, a Henley regatta badge and a copy of my father's funeral service – in the no man's land at the back of my desk drawers. Simon was a friend of my brother's until Simon met me and forgot that Stephen ever existed.

Like the rest of my lovers, I didn't care about him at all.

Do you know, Tessa, my darling, that although we've only known each other for seven weeks now (to the day – 49 days, there, that sounds better, nearly 50 days of our lives) I feel as though I've been fucking you all my life. And it's odd to feel that there was actually a first time and that it wasn't that long ago. How much is my memory distorted by hindsight? It seems to me that I remember feeling right from the beginning that something big was happening. Really I hardly knew you at all at that time. I was fucking someone who was virtually a stranger; and yet that stranger was you. That's a curious feeling, to think that I was fucking a stranger who was you. It seems rather dangerous in retrospect. I feel I want to travel back in time and watch over it to make sure I'm treating you right.

The first time Simon made love to me was on the floor of the playroom at the top of the old house. I had taken him up there with an offer of table tennis. I remember how the sun splashed through the leaded windows on to the wooden floor as we played game after game. It was hot, so I took off my cardigan.

Propped up against the wall by the window was an enormous gilt mirror in front of which I used to play dressing-up games, before life itself became so inventive. In front of that mirror I had practised – as a gypsy, a poker player, a charming burglar – the skills I was putting to good use as I flirted with the charming Simon Knight. I was fourteen. He was twenty-one, just down from Cambridge with a first-class physics degree, like my brother. That morning, before Simon came round looking for Stephen, I had stood in front of the mirror and seen myself amid the dark shadows of the tarnished glass. I remember thinking how much the glass had darkened over the years. I was nearly engulfed by the stain but I could make out the strong green eyes, the auburn hair tied back in a plait, the confident tilt to my hips and that slight smile.

The playroom had black swing doors like a saloon and a shaky balcony, from which I could almost touch the fir tree which blocked the light from one side of the house. My bedroom, my lovely lilac bedroom, was over the other side. Every morning during the summer holidays I would lie in bed for hours, reading and watching the squirrels playing along the limbs of the weeping willow outside my window. It irritated me when Simon Knight started phoning me every morning and interrupting my peace. He always asked me what I was reading and that somehow made it worse. He clearly knew he was disrupting me. He even began to recommend novels to me.

But I liked his letters and I liked the parties he took me to, where I was a star turn because of my youth and presumably my sexual attractiveness. Men would cluster round me and become very flustered and over-talkative. Women glared from corners. And I didn't do anything but stand there and smile. At times, I remember, I felt gloriously happy.

Simon began to get jealous after an undergraduate at one of these parties invited me to an Oxford ball.

'You're far too young,' he said in his car on the way home from the party. 'I'm not going to let you go.'

I turned to him, and smiled. 'Mind your own bloody business,' I said.

There was surprise and hurt on his broad face, as though I had just slapped him.

I kissed him on the cheek and ruffled his hair when we arrived outside my house. He remained very stiff. He dropped me off at the dark porch and roared off in his ridiculous red sports car.

Fortunately my parents slept soundly. I crept up the stairs to the solitude of my own room.

The next day, as I lay in his arms after he had made eager love to me in one of the musty bedrooms at the top of our house, I told him that I did not want to see him again.

'What do you mean?'

'What I say.'

He began to shake. The whole of his large body was trembling. I felt very distant from his distress, as I felt distant when we made love. It was all of no real consequence to me. It did not touch me. There was sweat on his forehead, on his hands, on the hairs which covered his body, in what I now considered a most unattractive way.

The bed we lay on was hard, with a dingy yellow cover embossed with horrid raised brown felt spots. There were cobwebs clinging to the edges of the small attic windows and just an old rug on the bare black boards. The one cupboard in the wall was very deep; it went back and back like a tunnel and was crammed with suitcases full of clothes my absentminded mother had forgotten.

'But I need you,' said Simon.

His skin felt cold and damp. He seemed to belong here, in this stale old room, like the other forgotten possessions.

I did not respond to his letters, or answer his phone calls, or take notice when my elder brother Stephen, who never asked me for anything, asked me to be kinder to his friend.

'I can't imagine why,' Stephen said, 'but it appears he's in love with you.'

Stephen towered above me. He is six foot four inches tall, with vast feet and hands. He has a low voice and brown eyes. Stephen is the one person, apart from myself, that I have always been afraid of, perhaps because he understands me better than anyone. My father persuaded him to be an astronomer because my father had always been interested in the stars; my father claimed that the more he knew of the universe, the more full of wonderment he became.

It was Stephen who told the news when, a month later, Simon was killed in a car crash.

'The police said it was an accident,' said Stephen, as he sat in the garden chair while I lay spreadeagled in my bikini beside him, sunbathing. I shielded my eyes from the sun as I looked up at him.

'Was anyone else hurt?'

'No, he was alone at the time.'

'That's awful. I do hope he was killed instantly.'

Stephen stood up and moved into a position where he blocked the sun from my body.

I scowled.

'Are you at all upset?' he asked. 'Simon was a nice chap, you know.'

'Of course I'm upset,' I said, turning onto my front, turning my back to him, wishing he'd get out of the way of the sun.

I could feel him staring down at me for a few seconds before he walked away.

I went to Simon's funeral because Stephen made me ('It's the least you can do'), and still have a copy of the service, which I keep with the rest of my memories in the drawers of this desk.

5

MARTIN SHERMAN

Sunday 3 September

TODAY I DRIFTED THROUGH THE HOUSE DAYDREAMING, washing up my breakfast bowl, dirtying another plate with baked beans on toast, not being bothered to wash that up, reading a science fiction story about mutants, staring out of the window, wondering which season I disliked most. And then I settled down to write this diary looking out over the Fields.

Highbury Fields tires me. There is always something going on: football, tennis, the circus, a fair, a cub fête. Other people, hellbent on pleasure, put up marquees, sell rock buns, rush about below me like mechanical toys well wound up. The enthusiasm with which most people approach life astounds me. They play tennis as if it mattered. They have picnics. They marvel at sunsets.

Sometimes I think I hate other people and that I have always hated them. I hate the way they try to make their futile lives important. At least I'm honest. At least I know it's all hopeless, pointless. Even this business of getting powerful is just a little board game to while away a few years between birth and death. And I know it's nothing to do with me really, just something I've been instructed to do by whoever or whatever throws the dice.

Often it seems that everyone else in the world has taken some course on how to live which somehow I've missed out on. But at other times I look up as I walk along a street and I see a face peering through a window, watching, envying me, thinking that I know the rules, that I have friends, lovers, perhaps a wife, that the heels of my shoes have been mended, that I get up in the morning without wondering why.

At least it will be November soon, the season of fires. On 5 November there is always a huge bonfire on Highbury Fields which shines red into the windows of the houses which flank the Fields.

I have just been for a walk and seen the sky streaked blue and pink. The clear air was cold and the dogs pranced and prowled and snuffled across the great green cloth. The grand houses linking the side of the grass faded until only their shape and the greeny-white hue of the painted windows remained.

A few lights were on, a few dinner parties in preparation. Men and women passing their lives in conversation, cutting up vegetables, passing vegetables, passing words backwards and forwards.

People get so absorbed by the existence in which they happen to be. Wherever they are, they think this is it. They don't see that they are just little plastic men and women seen from a great distance. They walk across the grass as though it has been here forever, as though they've been here forever, and will continue to be here forever. They have dinner parties as though they have always done so and will continue doing so forever. And yet it could all disappear so quickly, in ice, in fire, in flood, in time.

There hasn't been a fire here for a while, and so they forget.

6

TESSA ARMSTRONG

Tuesday 5 September

I AM SCARED. ALEXANDER BARTLEY, THE MAN WHO HELPED me kill my father, came into the estate agent's where I work this morning.

I had always feared that I would see Alexander again some time. He is a journalist, on the same Sunday paper as my father was, with offices just ten minutes from where I work. After my father died, my mother got a new job and moved to this area. I wish we had moved elsewhere.

Alexander Bartley still looks like a fallen angel with his fair hair and with his flushed cherub face sagging into a double chin.

I think he saw me. He left the office quickly.

He had been my father's best friend for a long time before he began to show an interest in me five years ago. They had covered Northern Ireland together, written major political pieces, even collaborated on a book about some murderer or other. Alexander was unscrupulous, clever and a liar; my father worked hard. They made a good team.

Most Sundays Alexander came over to Wimbledon with his family – a little boy and girl and a severe wife who, in common with a number of people, thought my vague, beautiful mother round the bend. Nevertheless, Alexander dumped his wife and went off to play tennis with my father.

My mother and Alexander's wife Sarah existed in completely different dimensions, and at times actually seemed invisible to each other. They would sit facing each other at the kitchen table and they would talk in turn in a desultory fashion but never gave the impression of addressing each other. Sarah would generally talk about her job as a lawyer and her problems with nannies while my mother, who is a botany teacher, would talk about subjects such as the mating habits of frogs.

The children, who were six and eight, with glasses and straight hair, would come and listen for a few minutes then rush out giggling. The two women never understood why.

Sometimes it seemed that my mother didn't understand anything. Tall, dreamy, with gorgeous creamy skin and fair hair always worn in a bun, she drifted through her days as though whatever she was doing was because she had temporarily forgotten what it was she was supposed to be doing. She ought to have lived in the country, in a big house, with plenty of children, and plenty of staff to look after her.

I can see her now collecting lilac blossom for the big vase in the sitting room. She is on tiptoe, in a cotton dress, her hair up in a bun, and she is cutting sprays of the flowers with a huge pair of scissors. I can almost smell the lilac. Almost, but not quite. The smell is out of reach, down a turning I can no longer find.

She lived in her private world, a good deal more attentive to her plants than she was to her husband, who treated her like a goddess. To him, she lived in a different, better dimension than his one of politics, informers and wars. He was even impressed by her ignorance.

On those Sundays Alexander and my father would return from tennis and request shandies, as though they had somehow behaved in a virtuous fashion demanding sympathy and attention from their wives. Sarah would always welcome them with relief while my mother floated off to the fridge and returned with a tray before vanishing, usually to her potting shed at the end of the garden.

I can still remember the light in the women's eyes when they saw Alexander coming through the door. And I remember my mother's eyes too, which would meet Alexander's before swerving away.

He would take little notice of the women but lounge about on the sofa, an overweight cherub, making remarks like 'It's good to do something for the family every now and again' as he drank his drink and smoked a cigarette. The self-congratulatory air which usually hung over Alexander at times became so intense that even I was irritated, and I liked Alexander: I liked his sauntering, mischievous quality; I liked his wicked chuckle which made his eyes squint; I liked the way he was completely selfish and yet managed to convince so many people that he cared for them. He made me laugh, too, because he took nothing seriously except himself and at times not even himself.

I remember the Sunday when I decided it would be amusing to make him fall in love with me.

It was the latest in a line of hot, dreary days. The papers had bored me except for a piece by Alexander on a Soho vice king. He wrote well in those days, with a sense of relish and excitement. My father often said that Alexander would be an editor of a national newspaper one day, and Alexander said the same about my father, but without the same sincerity. My father often joked admiringly about Alexander's womanizing, clearly accepting Alexander's opinion of himself as a great lover.

From my bedroom that afternoon I watched the two men out in the garden, lounging on deck chairs, and saw Alexander's shoulders shaking conspiratorially as he no doubt related another of his amatory adventures.

Alexander had known me so long, since I was eight, that he never took any notice of me. I wondered how long it would take to infatuate him. I left my desk, this desk, where I had been sitting and watching. I went over to my mirror. In a moment I changed my expression from that of a bright fifteen-year-old schoolgirl to that other look, and as I did so my eyebrows seemed to become darker, heavier, and my lips fuller, while my eyes opened wide, until I could see I was beautiful.

And then I smiled.

I changed into my shortest skirt and went down the staircase.

In bare feet on the cool grass I wandered over to where my father and Alexander sat. I felt particularly desirable that day. I remember being aware of the whole garden – the hedgehog who lived under the hedge which lined the right-hand side of the lawn, the lilac tree, the damson hollyhocks, the lavender bushes from which I used to make my lavender bags, the smell of sweet peas, the pleasant wet smell of the compost heap, and everywhere the air odd and sultry as though this rectangle, cloistered by bushes, hedges, fir trees, was somehow enchanted.

'Hello, Tessa. How's school?' said Alexander, pouring himself another shandy without looking at me. I'm sure that up until that day he wouldn't have recognized me if he'd seen me out of context, on the street, at a party. I was just a blur to him, someone who was the daughter of his friend and admirer.

'It's the holidays,' I said, folding myself down cross-legged in front of him in one fluid movement. I began to pluck daisies from the lawn.

'You're lucky to have a proper garden to play in, my girl,' he was saying. 'I was just telling your father how I envied his suburban life – park just nearby, lawn mowers humming, tennis down the road, decent people everywhere.'

I looked up, met his eyes, and smiled.

I hadn't realized it would be quite so easy.

My father was telling him how excellent his piece on the Soho vice king had been and Alexander, for once, wasn't listening to the praise. He was watching me continue to make my daisy chain and the expression on his face was that of a child at a sweet shop, half dazzled, half greedy, full of longing. It was actually rather a nicer expression than his usual smug one and it made me understand why women cared for Alexander.

For a week or two nothing happened. Then one morning, the day my father left for an investigation up in Scotland, I had a phone call.

'Tessa?' inquired a brisk female voice.

'That's right.'

'It's Amanda Curren here. We've heard you might be a suitable model for a fashion feature the paper's doing on the modern schoolgirl. Are you interested?'

I had taken the phone by the big stone fireplace in which my mother kept a vase full of ghastly pampas grasses.

'Oh yes. Certainly,' I said, stretching out my bare feet luxuriously and knocking feathery bits of pampas on to the fireplace below.

I knew quite well who would be writing the feature.

He came to pick me up in his electric-green monster of a car especially imported from America. I watched him from my parents' bedroom window as he got out of the car and patted down his hair with that smug ladykiller look. It was a coolish day and he was wearing a brown velvet jacket, which he clearly thought dashing. He strutted to the porch and rang the bell.

I hurried down, wide-eyed, in jeans and a shirt, my long hair carefully tousled, my face laboriously made-up to look unmade-up. Shyly, I opened the door, and at the sight of me Alexander's smugness lurched out of his face and was replaced by what in anybody else I would have called bashfulness. Then he seemed to recollect himself, remind himself that he was the clever, talented, charming future newspaper editor and I was just a schoolkid whom he was going to seduce. His shoulders moved around a bit as though trying to get the bad old Alexander operating smoothly. He smiled his 'I'm going to make you a star' smile. I smiled back.

On the journey to the paper he drove abominably and behaved worse. About five times he made the point that he had suggested me as a model for the feature. Three times he told me how the session could lead on to big things for me. Once he had the nerve to tell me how well the job would pay. He was so pleased at his cunning that he kept smiling to himself.

We drove past the Houses of Parliament, through Trafalgar Square, up Charing Cross Road, and he pointed out the National Gallery and Foyle's bookshop to me as though I were a naive little girl who'd only just arrived in the world, whereas I knew I'd existed since the beginning of time.

He guided me up the stairs with his hand resting possessively on my arm.

The fashion editor's office looked like a deserted jumble sale. Every available surface was strewn with coats, dresses, hats – while the adjoining room was that of a shoe fetishist – high-heeled, low-heeled, leather, sequinned, green plastic, every size and every shape and colour. Both rooms were empty of people except for two shop dummies standing by the dusty window of the main office. One wore just a baggy pair of flannel trousers and a checked scarf while the other wore nothing at all except a big straw hat. They had nippleless breasts and staring faces.

Alexander glanced at his watch and said, in a self-satisfied tone, 'The fashion staff must all have gone to lunch.'

'What a pity,' I said, and for a moment it seemed that all this had happened to me before – the dummies, the grey light from the unwashed windows, the metal desks piled with coats, the fallen angel of a man, my father's friend, standing with his back to the closed door, watching me intently.

I smiled at him.

I could hear the people passing in the corridor. I heard the clock tick. I could hear the rumble of traffic.

The door behind Alexander opened and the fashion editor undulated into the room like a black adder.

Alexander tried to fix his besotted expression back into wry cynicism and ended up with the most peculiar look.

'Hi, kids,' exclaimed the fashion editor. He put his hand on a leather-clad hip. 'And *what* is going on here?' In a smooth movement, graceful as a ballet dancer, he peered into Alexander's smitten face. Then he followed the direction of Alexander's gaze and, with theatrical flourish, threw up his hands.

'Why – if it isn't little Miss Lolita.'

I smiled.

'Don't try to vamp me, darling. But I must say, you do have a sensational smile.'

'Ray, I don't want you to photograph her after all,' said Alexander woodenly. 'All the men in England would be in love with her.'

'And does Lolita have a say in this?' Ray motored towards me.

'I don't care whether I'm photographed or not.'

'All you want is Alexander, right? How touching.' Ray took the straw hat off the dummy and placed it on his head. He assumed the pose and expression of a Southern belle.

We exchanged glances of mutual dislike and respect.

Alexander and I had lunch in a discreet Italian restaurant off Smithfield market. Before going in, we watched men in blood-spattered overalls carrying great carcasses of meat.

Over lunch he asked me about my school, my hobbies, my favourite pop stars. I answered his questions briefly, knowing that all men, but especially Alexander, like to talk, not to listen. And the subject dearest to Alexander's heart was himself so I made sure that our conversation didn't waver much from his opinions, his ambitions, his achievements. By the crème caramel (he chose cassata) he was even more in love with me. His eyes shone. I could almost see his heart leaping and turning.

I knew he was caught now, so I relaxed a little and became myself.

Later he said solemnly, 'What a very special lunch this has been.'

I darted him a quick glance and realized that he was perfectly sincere.

'Tessa, can we go for a walk in Hyde Park? You see, I want very much to kiss you.'

I looked down and strained to fabricate a blush. 'I can't, honestly. I promised my mother to get home by four-thirty and it's nearly four now.'

He took my hand.

'Then when can I see you again? I'm afraid I'm going to be in Belfast this weekend.'

I looked up – all eagerness. The eyes which met mine surprised me. They were very gentle.

'Oh – let me come too,' I said.

He frowned. 'I can't take you there, Tessa. I'm working.'

'Don't work. We could go to another hotel – not the one you and Daddy go to. The paper could send someone else to do the work, surely?'

'And what would you tell your parents?'

'That I'm staying with a friend in Westminster.'

'You're sure you'd get away with it?'

I nodded.

'You really want to go that much?'

I nodded again, letting my hair tip over my face a little, as wide-eyed and courageous as an Angela Brazil heroine.

'It's dangerous.'

'I know. That's why I want to go. And of course to spend a whole weekend with you. Oh please, Alexander.'

'I really shouldn't take you. Your father would never forgive me.'

'Oh *please*. We could have such fun – miles away from every-one. You could show me round Belfast.'

'I could, couldn't I?' he said to himself.

That weekend, as the taxi took us to the hotel, Alexander gave me a running commentary which related Belfast to the various news stories he had written and what the editor had said about them. While nodding and making appropriate noises I saw in my mind television newsreels I thought I'd forgotten. I saw adolescents and children with mouths open, throwing stones. I saw IRA men in black hoods like hangmen walking beside a coffin.

'Yes, I must admit, I really do think I've done some of my best work here,' he said as he handed the unshaven driver his fare.

The hotel room was spartan and clean with a good view of the cursed city. I stood looking down at the streets and buildings smudged by the rain as Alexander kissed my neck and fondled my clothed body in that desperate way men have. His hands were soon undoing the buttons of my shirt, then the buttons of my skirt. Next my bra was off – accompanied by a moan from him – then my pants were off and my stockings too and I stood naked in the grey light, facing the city, as Alexander's hands roamed over my buttocks while he made little gasping noises as though he had never felt anything more wondrous in his life than my small bottom.

He pulled me over to one of the twin beds with its orange cover, more or less pushed me down, and made love to me so quickly that it hurt a little when he entered me. But I didn't mind. I almost respected him for not messing around with my needs. It made me desire him a little. He cried out in enormous relief as he came. For a moment afterwards he lay so still and heavy on top of me that I thought he was dead. Eventually, he stirred.

'That was the best fuck in my life,' he murmured, and started to do it again. He made love to me four times that afternoon and I got quite to like his skin which, although flabby in places, was pleasantly soft and warm, like the skin of a woman. He had a nice, obliterating way of kissing too. His lips seemed to suck my whole mouth into his.

That evening, rather wearily, we explored the streets. We saw the Catholic tower blocks on hills overlooking the city. We saw metal barriers disfiguring the shops. We sat in dark wood pubs drinking Guinness and listening to the babble of the Irish men. But everywhere there were more solitary, less sociable figures standing on the fringes of things.

'Well, what did you think of Belfast?' he asked, as I brushed my hair at the dressing table watching us both reflected in the looking-glass. Alexander was sitting slumped on the bed naked, his belly corrugated into folds of fat. My eyes were big – excited, saucer eyes – and for a moment they seemed to me grey like the city.

'Beautiful,' I replied, smearing blood-red lipstick on to my lips.

The television set in the next-door room was babbling on about other wars in other places.

That other look took over Alexander's face – the quiet, penetrating one which made him a good journalist. He seemed to be staring into my soul.

My good mood vanished.

Suddenly the room seemed dark, as though the windows were letting the city, with its black hoods and black corners full of guns, into our room.

'You're a very curious girl. Sometimes I don't quite understand why I'm as much in love with you as I am,' he said.

'Don't love me,' I said.

He frowned. 'Why do you say that?'

'I'm too old for you.'

'You're only sixteen.'

'Fifteen actually,' I said.

'You told me…'

I shrugged and grinned.

He stood up slowly and went over to the window to close the curtains and cut out the dark, restless city.

He moved behind me and caressed my shoulders, massaging them as his eyes closed in pleasure.

I turned and made love to him with my mouth as the television in the room next door roared with canned laughter.

Downstairs, we both picked at our prawn cocktails. He looked exhausted and a little anxious. He quickly drank three double gin and tonics before going on to the wine, and the customary pink colour returned to his cheeks, once more those of a man well pleased with himself and his position in life. He wore his dark-blue velvet suit, one of a series of velvet suits designed to set him apart from other shabby, older journalists.

I wore a purple silk dress.

'There's too much glass in this hotel,' said Alexander. 'It'll get smashed by a bomb one day.' He pushed his fairish hair from his forehead upon which someone seemed firmly to have drawn three small lines.

There are some people who are born to be young and do not look good old. I could see other signs of age on Alexander – the shadows under the eyes, the lines splaying down from the nose, the thinning hair. Even his suit was a little threadbare in places. When the characteristic wicked twinkle left his eyes he just looked like a young person gone bad from too much food, drink and too many cigarettes. I doubted if I would continue my affair after the weekend. If I was going to have an affair with a middle-aged man I would find one whose proper age was middle age, not someone who'd stumbled there by mistake and who every now and again looked alarmed to have done so, alarmed not still to be a clever head boy with sunny curls and a way with girls.

'So,' he said, 'what's your analysis of the Irish problem, Miss Armstrong?' The side of his mouth lifted patronizingly. He had seen my expression cool on him and was trying to regain control. His face puffed up like a courting frog.

Instead of politely floundering and increasing his stature, I talked about the Irish situation while he slowly deflated.

He gave me his most direct and respectful look yet. 'You're clever, aren't you? Your father told me you were.'

I shrugged. 'My father's silly about me.'

'He thinks the world of you.'

I did not reply that I loved my father too, because I didn't realize then that I did. I thought I loved no one. Perhaps love is too simple a word for what I felt for my father, or maybe it's not the right word at all. What he did was fill my life with a certain strength. Above all, I suppose, my father had hope, and that is what I needed from him most of all (I wish my mother would stop playing that radio so loudly in her bedroom. It stops me thinking clearly. Perhaps she is planning what she will wear for her lover the next time she sees him. She makes herself ridiculous. She diminishes my father's memory, and herself).

Anyway, at the hotel in Belfast with Alexander I ordered steak, he ordered plaice. The waiter cleared away our prawn cocktails and sideplates and was just serving us with overcooked broccoli which sagged in silvery dishes like bits of green rag. It was past 10 p.m. and the half-empty restaurant was getting ready to close. The table beside us was being cleared away with a clanking of cutlery. The head waiter was leaning back on his heels, staring out of the window at the fading lights of the city. Everything and everyone seemed very still, as though waiting for something to happen.

For a minute or two there was a complete silence, as though the city had stopped, the talking had stopped, as though the frame of a film had frozen.

And then my father's voice rang out: 'Alexander!'

Alexander lost his alcoholic flush at once.

'Don't look round,' Alexander told me. He tried to smile at my father. It was only a half-smile, as if hoping that my father might not have recognized him after all.

I gazed at Alexander's corpse-like face with its demented smile.

'Go into the cloakroom,' ordered Alexander.

But it was too late. A few of my father's huge strides had taken him right behind me.

'Well, well,' boomed my father.

Usually such a greeting would have brought a boyish smirk to Alexander's eyes, a slight shaking of the shoulders, perhaps a wink. But he just stared at my father open-mouthed. He was a huge toy someone had left in the chair. His limbs fell loosely, his mouth fell, his body drooped. He no longer had any bones.

My father must, I thought, have assumed he was with a prostitute, and ashamed to be so. Politely he did not attempt to look at my face and clearly did not recognize me from behind in my tight purple dress, my hair up in a bun.

'So this is why you're skulking here – and not in the Europa as usual, heh?'

'Well, yes. I thought I'd take a weekend off,' replied Alexander's quavery voice.

'What? You lazy bugger. There's lots to do.'

There was a cold tone to my father's voice I had not heard before.

It was then that I wanted to cough. I tried very hard to stop myself, as though knotting tight string around my throat.

Alexander marshalled his forces. He inserted a knowing expression into his eyes.

'Look, Tom, give me a break.' And he winked.

It was a wink which suggested he was in the middle of a crucial chat-up sequence.

I felt I was being strangled by my need to cough.

'Ah ha,' said my father, and took a step back. 'Well, what about a drink, just the two of us, at the Europa tomorrow – say about eleven? I've something I want to talk to you about.'

'Right,' said Alexander.

I heard my father walk away.

I could not hold on much longer.

'He's going,' whispered Alexander, with a fixed smile.

With an enormous sense of relief, I coughed.

Alexander's fixed smile hardened and his eyes protruded. 'He's stopped,' he said, hardly moving his lips.

I stared at Alexander in horror.

'He's coming back,' said Alexander, still smiling. 'He looks as though he's going to kill someone.'

My father's great voice roared, 'Tessa!'

I turned round.

For a moment, everyone in the restaurant stopped eating. A trolley of puddings was halted, forks were held halfway to mouths, the anxious head waiter loitered close by muttering to himself.

My father was standing by us with his legs wide apart like some mighty giant.

'Is there an explanation?' he boomed.

A blonde girl and an old man got up and left. The others returned politely to their food and conversation. A man with a big nose took out a handkerchief and wiped it anxiously.

Alexander's face was yellowy.

'Look, Tom…' he said in a thin, low voice which was aiming at a man-to-man tone. 'Your daughter. She's not a little girl any more, you know.'

There was a second's pause before my father let out a yell of rage.

He grabbed him by the collar, drew him up, and hit him.

Alexander was thrown back against a pillar, like a toy again, but a toy with an expression of immense surprise.

My father lurched towards him.

Alexander's surprise altered to anger.

Alexander's flaying fists sent my father hurling back into a steel trolley.

47

My father hit his head on the side of the trolley and collapsed.

I looked quickly at Alexander, and for a moment I could have sworn I saw satisfaction on his features.

Alexander whispered urgently, 'Get out of here at once.'

An hour later I was on a plane.

As I flew out of Belfast airport I kept seeing again the pleasure on Alexander's face, and I saw again and again my father's big face, drained of colour, already dying.

From the plane everything looked very small, very inconsequential. I told myself it didn't matter. My father would be all right.

My father died around 3 a.m. in hospital. My mother did not get there in time. I should have stayed.

No one, to my knowledge, ever found out I had been in Belfast that evening. I said I had been staying with a friend in London.

It was reported that Tom Armstrong had been accidentally killed in a brawl with his fellow journalist over a story. The prostitute with whom Alexander had been dining at the time vanished and had not been able to be traced to give evidence. He had never seen her before that weekend.

My problem was that, for the first time in my life, something mattered.

For days, I could not stop crying.

My mother, however, did not seem grief-stricken by my father's death. She just seemed surprised. Even at the cremation she wafted into the chapel looking as lovely as usual, merely a little more confused. She nodded at the friends crowding the small building as though not absolutely sure why they were there.

She sat next to me on the hard wooden seats with her long hands on her lap. I remember she smelt of some new scent.

I wished I could tell her what I had done. I remember thinking it was braver to keep it to myself, and at that time it was important to me that I should be brave, like my father.

She wore a pale-blue striped dress and hat, as if she were at a wedding. She looked very lovely, very much the beautiful widow.

On her other side sat my brother. He stared fixedly in front when he wasn't praying fervently or singing lustily. But afterwards, as we stood around the wreaths, he kept glancing down at my red-eyed face with a mixture of puzzlement and revulsion, as though he knew what had happened, although there was no way he could have known.

For once, outside in the courtyard, my brother and I were both appalled by the same thing. Alexander Bartley had sent a bouquet of flowers, a vast pile of brownish-purple and yellow orchids which dominated the other flowers and wreaths like some decayed angel of death.

My mother couldn't stop looking at them.

'Most interesting,' she said to no one in particular. 'Lady's Slipper you know.' She was smiling to herself.

'They're disgusting,' said Stephen. 'Can't she see? He shouldn't have sent them.'

'She finds them botanically interesting,' I replied.

'She has a silly look on her face,' remarked Stephen. 'She should at least *try* to pull herself together.'

Some female journalist came simpering up to Stephen who stooped down politely to hear her pert questions about his job as an astronomer.

My mother's lovely voice drifted on about orchids while others moved miserably from foot to foot as though trying to keep out the cold, although it was a warm day there, in those sheltered gardens with their neatly crimped lawns and their pruned rose bushes representing dead souls.

'Orchid flowers are extraordinary... diversity of colour and form... basically three sepals and three petals... take on the most bizarre shapes and hues... used in food and drink as aphrodisiacs... Lady's or Aphrodite's slipper, you know...'

49

The next day my mother insisted I help her clear my father's things from her room. We knelt on the floor in front of their wardrobe and piled his shoes into a big plastic bag for a jumble sale. The heels were hardly worn at all. 'He was always very light on shoes,' she said, pushing her hair back from her pale face, and I imagined him dancing along the road, hardly touching the ground, so full of buoyancy that he disobeyed gravity.

Then I saw him lying on the floor of that hotel restaurant, with a face made of chalk, dying.

Involuntary sobs kept breaking out like painful hiccups. I was sorry for him, of course, but I was more sorry for myself and what I might become.

My mother watched me. She didn't touch me. She didn't put her arms around me. She just sat – one of the beautiful cloth dolls my father used to bring me back from his trips abroad. I noted that she was wearing crimson lipstick, and that her nails were manicured. Far from his death making her neglect herself, it had had the opposite effect. She behaved like a woman who had been freed.

I dragged myself up and staggered away from her with my arms out in front of me, a blind person.

The following day we packed his diaries and letters away too, up in the attic along with the dolls he'd given me, the toys, the dressing-up box.

We packed my father's papers in an old leather suitcase which had belonged to his father.

I haven't ever dared look at them in case they told me things about him, and about me, that I didn't want to know.

They sit up there, acquiring dust, turning grey.

I wish my mother would turn down her ridiculous music. She plays it loud, like a teenager. Since my father's death she has become younger and younger and I have become old.

I should be the one playing loud music, having love affairs.

7

Martin Sherman

Wednesday 6 September

I AM WRITING THIS DIARY ON THE FORMICA-TOPPED TABLE
which serves as my desk. It is shoved up against the window
from which I see the trees in the breeze and the people passing
below. Because the windows are very dirty all the colours are
muted. Some of the leaves have already fallen and lie curled up
like clenched fists.

I might have known I'd meet her in the autumn.

Today was cold and bright, too cold for this time of year, which
should be a mellow type of summer, not a sunny form of winter.

Even before I saw her, I felt exhilarated. I like this season. I like
to watch the vigour with which things die.

I brushed down my slightly shabby coat and wandered into
the estate agent's office. You see, after my dream about the devil,
I know I am going to become rich. He is going to make me rich,
and he is going to make me powerful. It's the old pact. People
enter into it all the time. But of course I have to find the means
to become rich. I decided that buying and selling property might
be amusing.

Behind a metal desk at the estate agent's a young man in a
swivel chair turned to face me with a smile which wrenched all
his small features. A nameplate on his desk announced that he
was Gerard Richardson.

I grinned back at him.

'I should like to see a maisonette please. I'd prefer one which has been tightly fitted into a house, if possible,' I said.

Mr Richardson smiled more fixedly.

The office was dotted with pot plants and painted a Regency green. Cork noticeboards sported artists' impressions of buildings as yet unbuilt. Everywhere there were black-and-white photographs bombastically defaced by the word 'sold' in red capital letters.

'That's an interesting request,' said Gerard Richardson.

His well-fitting suit had a faint sheen. He wore a colourful tie.

On his round, flat face a bad craftsman had moulded a tiny nose and stuck little currant eyes. His mouth was made of matchsticks, two thin lines. And yet he had a certain odd charm, an eagerness to please.

'I like a resourceful use of space,' I explained. 'As many rooms tucked into as small an area as possible.'

'I see,' said Gerard Richardson, his weasel face attempting to imitate respect. 'Usually people want a lot of space, not a little, for their money. But I'll certainly do my best to get you just what you want. That's my business.'

At that moment there was a laugh from the end of the room where an elderly woman sat with her back to us. She had a thick plait of long grey hair, and a cardigan hanging over her shoulders like a shawl. She was small, and sat up very straight. What was odd about her was her laugh. She appeared to be an old lady but it was the laugh of a young girl, a high silvery noise, ringing like a coin through the stuffy office.

Mr Richardson's face darkened.

'That girl,' he muttered.

I smiled sympathetically but was confused as to why Mr Richardson, who was not, after all, much older than I, should refer to a little old lady as a girl.

With pursed lips, he pushed at a pile of papers on his desk as though wishing to push the woman off a cliff.

'Houses,' I said to remind him. 'Resourceful use of space.'

He jumped up. 'Of course. Of course.'

He threw his head back and scuttled like a wind-up toy to the filing cabinet where at top speed he rifled through a drawer calling out streets and prices. He seemed nervous.

There is something about me which disconcerts people. Perhaps they sense my underlying insolence. I suspect they think I'm the type who knifes people. Mr Richardson seemed to – he kept glancing round at me furtively.

'Gorgeous little house just round the corner from here – it might be just the thing for you.'

He had one hand on his hip.

Through the large window at the front of the office I could see the sky hard and blue.

Mr Richardson had, I considered, learnt all his lines properly and noted how real people behave so that now he did a good impersonation of a rather camp estate agent. Until recently I, who am probably at least as empty as Mr Richardson, could not be bothered to learn the lines. I have always been in the audience, a figure without identity munching crisps and watching other people live or pretend to live.

I took the house details from him, two stapled sheets of paper.

'A bit on the expensive side for me at present,' I said convivially.

He blinked at me. What was I doing wrong? My coat was shabby but not too shabby, surely? I was saying the right words, surely. How was it that people could tell I didn't belong?

He turned back to his filing cabinet and continued to call out prices and places.

I don't know why it was that I began to stare at her shoulders.

I don't know why it was that I began to feel very hot. Suddenly my clothes stuck to me the way they do through stifling summer nights. I could feel the sweat on my skin.

'Too expensive!'

'Too cheap!'

'Not enough rooms!' I called out.

'Three bedrooms, not far from the canal...' Mr Richardson was saying.

The door opened and a man with a florid face entered.

'I must go,' I said, suddenly filled with an unaccountable panic. I put my hands in my pockets and tried to move.

Mr Richardson blinked at me, with a puzzled expression.

The florid gentleman whose cheeks were puffed out like two small red balloons sat down at the desk facing Mr Richardson's and began to study some papers in front of him.

'Cold out,' he said, to no one in particular. 'Very brisk.'

'Don't you want to take some of these house details?' asked Mr Richardson peevishly.

I still couldn't move. My gaze had returned to the old lady.

The draught from the red-faced man's entrance had made me shiver, and I was still shivering. I wished for a moment I were back in the supermarket, in my other guise, in my uniform, striding up and down the alleyways piled high with brightly coloured goods, playing at stacking tins into pyramids, arranging the special-offer packets, watching out for her, lost in a maze of my own making.

At least I was safe there.

'Ah now! At last,' cried Mr Richardson. 'I have the very thing for you. It's in Cloudesley Street. Three bedrooms, a small bathroom, a living room and a kitchen off, on two floors.'

The glare of the supermarket was different from the glare of this office with the daylight screeching down onto the grey metal desks.

I looked away from the old lady and saw myself in a big square mirror. I experienced the familiar shock at my unruly red hair, my clear blue eyes, my delicate pointed face. I did not feel like this person. I felt suddenly tiny, desperate, lonely, full of unresolved desire.

I brushed at the collar of my jacket, removing a non-existent bit of fluff.

When I looked back the old lady had turned towards me, and our eyes met. She wasn't an old lady.

She was about twenty, with arched eyebrows, wide eyes which reminded me of that creepy kind of stillness before thunder broke out, and a scornful, somewhat arrogant expression. Her face was thin and her cheekbones high.

But her lips made up for the hardness in her face: they were full, voluptuous, radiant.

She sat gracefully, very pert and straight, like a prima ballerina, with her head turned to watch me.

There was a curious darkness about her. Not just because of the long rope of grey hair which contrasted oddly with her youthful marble skin, stray wisps framing her face like something out of a spiritualist's photograph album.

It was her smile which was extraordinary. It was quite savage. It seemed to be mocking everything. And yet even in mocking everything, especially all the usual reasons people smile – the lust, the friendship, the love – it brought them all to my attention, summoned them all to her feet.

She was very beautiful, and yet not really beautiful at all. Somewhere in her lips, in her eyes, in the landscape of her face, there were black caves I didn't wish to approach, that reminded me of things I wished to forget – of nightmares, of the corners of rooms, of turnings into dark alleyways, of women crying, and of the beginning and the end of things.

And then her expression softened and the caves disappeared and suddenly I was looking straight at her lips, slightly parted, while her eyes danced with light and mischief.

'Hello,' I said.

'Hello,' she replied, very clear and bright.

I knew it was she, of course.

She was like looking at my own self: some part of me I hadn't known existed, something merrier and more wicked and much more dangerous.

She turned briskly back to what she was doing, just a typist again, leaving me swaying slightly.

'Reginald will take you round to Cloudesley Street if you'd like to go,' said Mr Richardson.

The florid-faced man looked up. 'Too busy,' he said, pushing out his cheeks like an oversize hamster with his cheeks full. With rounded shoulders, he huddled protectively over the bits of paper on his desk.

I glanced at my watch.

'I must go.'

'It's very reasonably priced. Very reasonable for what it is,' said Mr Richardson.

I wished she'd look round again.

Even her skin was odd, dreamy, not quite real.

'Would you like to see the property another time, sir?'

'Yes. Absolutely... er... tell me, how many flats in the house?'

'Two maisonettes and one flat.'

'That's pretty good going in one of those thin houses,' I said.

'The price reflects the compactness of the property, sir.'

'Could I see it on Saturday?'

'Certainly, sir.'

'Perhaps the young lady could take me.'

I saw her shoulders tense.

'Of course, sir.'

'About eleven would be best.'

'Tessa, you're taking this gentleman...'

'Martin Sherman...' I said, staring at her back, wanting the words to sink into her consciousness.

'You're taking Mr Sherman to that Cloudesley Street place at eleven o'clock, sharp, Saturday.' He hurled the words over at her as though trying to knock her down. She was sitting, very self-contained. He was one of those small, fussy men who don't like any women except their mothers and whom most women dislike. Certainly Tessa gave the impression that she would have liked each tap at her keyboard to have been a gunshot directed at Mr Richardson.

His office was tidy without being stylish.

He had white chrysanthemums on his desk, which he probably thought rather dashing, but they made the room smell acrid. Some of the pot plants were sickly creatures browning at the corners.

There were no windows open.

'Will that be OK?' I said to her.

I noted her nameplate – 'TESSA ARMSTRONG' – on her desk.

Reginald Thomas sniffed and Mr Richardson took out a packet of vitamin C tablets from his top left-hand drawer and started to swallow them one after the other while watching Reginald Thomas malevolently.

Mr Thomas blew his nose and Mr Richardson winced.

Tessa continued to type as though she hadn't heard me.

'Will that be OK?' I asked again, moving closer to her until I was standing over her.

Her long white hands rested for a moment on the keys.

I think she was wearing a black skirt and beige woollen cardigan over her shoulders but the impression she gave was all grey.

She looked up.

'Probably,' she said, and then swept her eyes down on to the rows of black text before her.

My skin was very hot again.

'Mr Sherman,' summoned Mr Richardson tetchily. 'Would you like to come here and fill in this form? We need to know your name, address, telephone number, number of bedrooms…'

I pulled myself away from Tessa and knew that I was pulling her with me.

I stood on the other side of the desk from where Mr Richardson was sitting demurely, compact as the flats he was offering, no extra space taken up by elbows or sprawling limbs or anything but the smallest of emotions. A certain petty crossness emanated from him that was all. Even his mouth was small.

Although I was large in size, for the last few years I had tried to stay unnoticed, out of the way, hidden in a Wendy house and a shop, but now I was breaking out and could feel my arms shoot out through the windows, my legs kick through the doors.

My breathing was irregular.

The girl would not look at me again, however hard I stared. She wrapped her shoulders round her like a cloak.

I wondered what she could be doing here. She didn't belong here either, in the dark end of the office, her beautiful face looking at a blank wall, her back to the customers, showing only her long grey braid.

It was stuffy. My clothes were sticking to me.

While Mr Richardson filled in his form, he kept glancing up as though my presence made him nervous.

'Thank you, Mr Sherman,' he said, when I had answered all his questions.

He stretched out with a precise movement to bring the glass ashtray in front of him. He was unwrapping his packet of cigarettes carefully. Now he was depositing the cellophane in the wastepaper basket beside him. He then swept his hand over the area of the desk where he had opened the packet, as though there might be a residue of dust. And then with pincer fingers he took out a cigarette, which he lit and took a drag as though it were his first one ever. He puffed at it like a child, holding it low down, near the filter.

'Sorry – you don't smoke do you, Mr Sherman?' he said, wanting me to go. Wanting my alarming presence out of his little domain.

I grinned. I was getting bored with being polite. But I knew I must behave myself. At the supermarket I am known for my rudeness and solitariness but always get away with things because I am useful and strong, and also because I can summon up easy charm when necessary.

'I'd better leave you in peace,' I told Mr Richardson. 'I have some important clients to see.'

He looked as though he almost believed me, but not quite. I could see I would have to polish up my act a little. Perhaps some new clothes, perhaps a haircut, certainly I would have to watch more closely how respectable young businessmen behaved, the lines they said, the tone they adopted.

Just Thursday and Friday to get through, two days of dreams and anticipation before Saturday, when I would see Tessa.

'Goodbye, Tessa.'

There was a short silence.

'Goodbye,' she said in a clear voice, and at once resumed her work.

As I stepped out into the street the sun was glittering over the pavement like gold dust.

8

Tessa Armstrong

Wednesday 6 September

TODAY A YOUNG MAN CAME IN – RED-HAIRED, FULL OF SWAG-
ger and wildness – and I experienced a moment of lust for the
first time in years. His name is Martin Sherman. I don't want this,
I don't want to return to what I was.

I left work early, complaining of a headache.

At home I sat up in my bedroom just staring out of the window,
and remembering, until the doorbell rang.

For a moment I was convinced it was him – Martin Sherman –
and my heart began to beat fast, in panic, I suppose.

I didn't answer the bell at first.

I stood up and walked to my mother's room, where I sat at the
dressing table and saw with alarm the face the mirror threw back
at me. If only I could have abandoned that face somewhere, buried
it under leaves one wet dark evening or thrown it into a dustbin
just before collection. I hated the way it watched me: from dark
windows, through mirrors, in the expressions of others. Pale and
possessive, my other self.

I reached out and smeared my mother's gloss on the lips of
the face.

In the mirror the face smiled and the full lips grew fuller.

The bell rang again.

I stood up, and went to the window.

I noted a white sports car parked outside. I felt sure that Martin would not own a white sports car. If he owned a car at all it would be old, with torn leather seats.

I walked down the stairs. It is a bare, silent house, bereft of connections. There are no photographs on the wall. No pictures of aunts or grandmothers. And nothing matches anything else. The curtains don't go with the walls and the walls don't go with the carpets. Everything separate, divided.

The hall is a dingy yellow. There are no coats, no umbrellas, no old newspapers. The telephone seldom rings. We are cut off from the past and the future. My mother said she'd redecorate the house, but except for her gaudy bedroom she left it as it was, someone else's dingy paint, someone else's splodgy curtains, carpets which strangers have walked on.

I opened the door.

'Why Tessa!' exclaimed Nicola Ward, who pushed by me. 'It's marvellous to see you.'

She threw her gloves onto the table below the hall mirror and took off her leather coat.

'I bet you weren't expecting me,' she said.

She swept into the drawing room, and switched on all the lights. She had been my best friend at school, the one I showed my letters to. But I hadn't seen her since she left school after the scandal which was, I suppose, my fault.

Slim legs, hair pitch-black, a suntanned face. Her back was to me as she ran her finger over the dust on the mantelpiece.

'I am so sorry to barge in. But I simply had to come to congratulate you.' She turned round, and a bright grin swung across her face. 'About your mother's forthcoming marriage.'

Everything fell silent.

She kept grinning.

'To whom?' I said in a small voice.

'I'm sorry, Tessa, what did you say?' she said.

'I said – who is she marrying?'

She was exultant but she tried not to show it. She clenched her hands as though to keep a hold on her delight.

'Oh – don't you know?'

Nicola has hated me ever since a hot summer's evening about six years ago, the evening I persuaded Nicola to come to a club with me, to pick up two boys. She was far more strait-laced than I, but eventually relented.

'Only I'm not bringing them back here, and we're not going back to their places,' she said (we were staying at her parents' house in Westminster while they were away for the weekend).

'Fine,' I had said, 'we'll just amuse ourselves for an hour or so then ditch them.'

We dressed, with the care and pleasure of adolescence, and went out, ready to enslave.

'What's your name?' my partner asked at the club.

My partner was not unattractive, I remember thinking, as he stood in front of me swaying his shoulders to the noise of the music and watching me. He had cropped hair and small, ardent eyes. His shoulders were quite wide.

I muttered my name shyly, simpering a little, and watched the effect.

He moved closer and his eyes grew smaller. 'What did you say, love?' He put his hot hands on my arms and bent nearer to me to hear my words through the loud drone of disco noise. He smelt pleasantly of sweat.

His friend, a less taut version of himself, was dancing with Nicola, his limbs all over the place. She was looking very prim and cross. Nicola hadn't wanted to come to this club in the first place because it was crowded and dark and not at all respectable.

'You been here much?' shouted my partner.

I shook my head, and smiled fatuously.

'Don't live in London,' I shouted.

He jerked his head towards Nicola.

'Your friend live here?'

I nodded, all smiles, all sweetness.

'Wanna go for a walk?'

At that moment, I swear it, I had no idea what I was planning. But I knew I did not want to be bored that evening. The week had been very dull. Schoolwork, no dramas, lukewarm weather.

This evening it was hotter than it had been for days, and that perhaps accounted for the pent-up atmosphere in the club.

'OK,' I said. 'I'll ask my friend.'

'Certainly,' said Nicola. 'Sooner the better. But not with these louts.'

'Mine's quite cute.'

She glanced at me suspiciously.

'Where do you want to go?'

'Just for a walk. Through London. Be fun.'

'Look – I don't like them.'

'You don't know anything about them.'

'You don't like them either. I can see. What are you playing at?'

'Let's just go then,' I sighed, as though admitting defeat.

I took Nicola by the arm and steered her away.

In the cloakroom, painted black and chipped, we each looked into a mirror. I saw that cold, glittering expression about my lips and eyes.

Nicola stared at her face with a kind of disappointment, although it was actually prettier than mine, with strong high cheekbones, fine eyes and a pouting little mouth. She smeared on some pink lipstick which matched her trousers and shirt.

Her skin was creamy, wholesome, whereas mine, in the half-light of the basement, had a glow which was almost unhealthy, as if belonging to this underworld of false flashing lights and black corners.

'Let's just go home now, shall we?' she said.

'Yes. Let's just walk back.'

Nicola went up the stairs first. She stopped at the top.

'Hello,' she said miserably.

As I had expected, they were waiting for us outside in the hot air of the Soho street, looking younger and more foolish than they had in the flattering throb of the club. Perhaps Nicola and I looked better outside, because the two boys seemed disconcerted, and uncertain about what to do with their feet.

'Well,' I giggled, glancing at Nicola, who scowled back murderously. 'What next?'

'What about going back to Jeff's place?' said my one, gesturing in Jeff's direction in case we weren't certain who he was referring to. My one, whose name was Mick, had an agreeable thuggish face even though it lacked the few years' ageing process which would have improved it. He was one of those men who are at their best around forty – stupid, set in their ways, but sexy. Jeff, however, looked as though his prime had been around three years old when his air of gormlessness might perhaps have been endearing.

'Well, I don't know about you, Tessa, but I'm going home,' announced Nicola, and started to walk off along the pavement. It was a tatty street with a few dustbins, Chinese restaurants, export dress shops and open doors which led up to the rooms of call girls. A cat ran across the road. It was summer, and a weekend, and it seemed that only tourists, cats and people like us looking for trouble remained in the city.

Mick caught Jeff's eye and then jerked his head towards Nicola. Jeff eventually got the point, and after a puzzled look at me, he sped off after Nicola while Mick turned to me.

'And where's her home?' he said, with renewed confidence, standing over me, close to me, with an intimate note to his voice.

'Westminster,' I replied, staring at the ground.

'Jeff lives in Lambeth. We could walk her home first.'

The evening was darkening and the air turning to soft velvet as the smells of dust and rotting fruit threw themselves like streamers through the city night.

'You'd better keep away from Jeff – he fancies you,' said Mick to me.

He put his arm around my waist with a kind of tough tenderness.

Some way in front, Jeff was trying to put his arm round Nicola. She was hurrying in front of him huffily.

'Does she really not like him – or what?' he asked.

'Oh she'll probably start to laugh soon, and enjoy herself. He is trying awfully hard.'

It was my longest speech.

He looked down at me, then looked away.

'You've got a nice face,' he said. 'It's very pretty.'

As we walked through Soho, down Charing Cross Road, out into Trafalgar Square, the air grew clammier. We passed the four huge black lions which guard London, we passed Nelson standing on his column bathed in a curious green light, we walked along Whitehall beside the Foreign Office, Downing Street, the great expanse of the Ministry of Defence – until we reached Parliament Square, with Westminster Bridge behind it, where I realized I had been aiming all along.

'I think it's going to thunder,' I said.

'Let's get a cab back,' said Nicola.

'I want to stand on the bridge,' I said.

Jeff was watching me as we stood, four small figures on the corner of Whitehall and Parliament Square.

'Let's go on the bridge, if she wants to.'

I could sense Nicola's mood tightening. She didn't want Jeff, but she resented his interest in me.

'All right then,' said Nicola, lurching forward with the unspoken words 'She always gets her way anyway – there's no use resisting'.

She led the way, head thrown back, a figure in pink: pink bottom, pink shirt, hair jet-black and tied in a plait like mine. A desirable figure, I would have thought. But the two young men walked beside me like guards and let her race on.

'There,' she said as we stood at the rails of the bridge, and the thunder began to rumble some way away. 'Isn't it marvellous? Look at the Houses of Parliament. Terrific, don't you think? The way some of it is illuminated, and the rest remains in the dark, like some mysterious forest. Didn't Wordsworth write a poem standing just here or was it somewhere else?

> *The world is too much with us; late and soon,*
> *Getting and spending, we lay waste our powers;*
> *Little we see in Nature that is ours;*
> *We have given our hearts away, a sordid boon.*

And look, look, Tessa; aren't those lights pretty – like necklaces along the banks of the Thames tied from lamppost to lamppost.

'Now is that OK? Is that all right? Can I go home now or is there something else you want us to do, somewhere else you wish us to go?'

She swung round at Jeff. 'Why don't you say something? Don't you know any poems?'

A few fat drops of rain were falling down and below the bridge the Thames flowed thick and dark, glossy with reflected lights. We were leaning on the wide grey railings and looking south.

He shook his head. Mick moved from foot to foot restlessly.

'The seat of power, that is. Did you know that? My father's an MP – you didn't know that, did you? Are you backing away?' She sidled up to Jeff, pushing her wet hair back from her face, and she gave Mick a quick glance, and quite a sexy smile.

'We should be getting back,' said Mick.

'Power is an ability to control other people and events. It is at times bought with money. Tessa is someone who was born with power. She can make people do what she wants. She could make either of you walk along this railing.'

She slapped the railing.

'She could make either of you walk, or indeed run, along here. You would clamber up – with the help of that lamppost and stand there, pleased, proud, to do what she wanted, and if you slipped you'd fall down into that black mass below.' She peered over. 'It looks rather like tar, doesn't it? But you probably wouldn't slip, because really it's rather wide and you two are young and probably have good balance. That's what power is, you know, what Tessa has. And power can be used for good or for evil or for either, as the whim takes one. People who have power – sexual, financial, political – often don't appreciate it. But those who don't have it suffer from their lack of consequence. It's not nice to be inconsequential. And I'm inconsequential compared to Tessa – and Jeff – you're inconsequential compared to Mick. It's tough – why do we do it to ourselves?' she asked Jeff. 'Why go around with people like Tessa and Mick? Because we are all drawn to power. That's why they're powerful. Now Jeff, would you get up on that railing for me, just for me?'

He shook his head, and put his hands in his pockets.

'There are no policemen around. It's too wet for them – see.' She pointed down at the water which was pockmarked with the rain.

The rumble erupted into thunder and I threw my face back, turning it up to the rain.

Nicola stared, hands on her hips.

'How come you turn everything into a drama starring you? How come as I stand here and declaim you throw back your head and the men watch you with longing? You're not even especially pretty. I mean, if you died you wouldn't look pretty, once the life had left your face, whereas I would still look pretty.'

'If I walk along that wall for you…' said Jeff's voice. 'The railings thing… will you sleep with me tonight?' he said to me.

I shook my head.

'Will you?' he asked Nicola.

She pursed her lips together so tightly that they nearly disappeared into her face. Her hands clenched into tiny tight balls of fury.

'If you run, quite fast.'

I laughed. I wanted to see what would happen. Lightning was illuminating the sky like fireworks and the Houses of Parliament looked hardly real, as though made of balsa wood.

Big Ben stood at 12.15 a.m.

Mick's arm tightened around me.

'I don't think you should…' Mick was saying.

'Shhh,' I said, and playfully touched him on the nose with my finger.

'But…'

Jeff was beginning to climb up on the railings.

I put two hands around the back of Mick's neck and pulled his lips down to me.

'I'm up,' yelled Jeff.

Mick pushed me away, and went towards Jeff, his hand out.

'Jeff – it's dangerous. Take care.'

'I want a fuck tonight,' shouted Jeff, looking at me. 'I'm all right.'

'Come down,' said Nicola.

'Look at me,' he said again and started to saunter along the edge.

A policeman was running along the pavement towards him.

'Stop that at once, get down,' he shouted.

With an expression of amazement which made his face for a moment enlarge in the dark night, Jeff swayed.

I can still remember him standing there swaying, his mouth and eyes wide open in a kind of glorious delight which was also terror. His trousers were slightly too long for him, I recall. Perhaps they had belonged to an elder brother. And his fake leather jacket was rather too big, especially round the sleeves. He had rather more hair than Mick but at the moment it wasn't the hair which was noticeable but the wet, glistening face with the neck tipped back as though trying to drink up all the rain.

As he fell he screamed but it sounded more like a battle-cry than a cry of fear.

Later, as we waited to be interviewed at the police station, Nicola accused me of making her encourage Jeff to walk along the railings.

'It was you,' she said. 'You caused his death.'

'Did I?' I asked Mick, placing my cheek on his shoulder.

'Of course not,' he said. 'Nicola did it. She virtually pushed him off. I'm willing to testify to that.'

'Please don't. Say it was an accident. For my sake,' I said.

He caressed my hair.

Nicola looked at me with a mixture of hate and gratitude which I found quite intoxicating.

Sullenly, from then on, she did whatever I asked.

But now she had come here, to my home, with her news of my mother, to collect her revenge.

She slunk elegantly into an armchair, her long legs crossed. She looked Italian, and far older than her twenty years.

'I said – don't you know who's marrying your mother?' Nicola repeated.

I smiled, and I saw again the expression with which the younger Nicola, the fifteen-year-old schoolgirl, used to look at me.

'Why are you smiling like that?' she said, and the wires which had joined her into a complete whole snapped.

I shrugged.

'Perhaps you don't believe me,' Nicola continued. 'I can assure you I'm right. She is getting married.'

'I'm sure you are.'

'I hear all about him from a journalist friend of mine. Geoffrey Reuter. He's a friend of your mother's fiancé.'

'He's your lover, is he?'

'That's right.' She yawned. 'Married of course… but aren't they always, all the nice men? He told me where you live.'

Her pretence at blasé sophistication didn't come off, as she couldn't stop watching me nervously, her eyes darting about in her head like terrified goldfish.

She forced herself to look down at her well-manicured nails.

'Have you heard that I got a scholarship to Oxford? All the same, I spend most of my time in London. I've done a number of features, for various papers… have you noticed?'

'I don't read the newspapers.'

Her face tightened with disappointment.

'By the way,' she said quickly, 'do you ever see anyone from school? Corinna? Sheila? Melanie?'

'I don't see anyone.'

'Are you surprised?' She stared at me brightly.

'About what?' I asked.

'That I've done so well.'

'Not in the least. You were always very single-minded.'

Nicola flushed with what I could have sworn was pleasure.

'Look, aren't you even going to offer me just a little cup of tea… after all this time?'

'No,' I said.

'But you want my news. You want to know who your mother is marrying, you want to know quite badly. I can see. I don't blame you. Give me a cup of tea and I'll tell you.'

'I don't want your news,' I said.

'You're trembling.'

'Please Nicola. Please leave me alone.'

She stood up slowly.

'We could be friends. After all, we were at school together. You've had a rough time. We've both had a rough time. After... that evening... I had a kind of nervous breakdown. And you... you've changed. But we could forget about it all.'

'I'm very busy at the moment. Would you mind going?' I said.

'As you please,' she said. She stood graciously up and stalked down the hallway, out of the front door, into the windy street, leaving behind her the strong smell of perfume, of worldliness, of all the things pulling me away from this room of mine with its desk and its diary.

As I stood in the hall listening to her car roar off I thought of Martin Sherman again, and the way his presence had filled the whole office, disturbing, disrupting with his worldliness. If I went to work I would see him again, this Saturday.

I want to see him. I am tired of these dreams and memories.

9

Martin Sherman

Thursday 7 September

Over the last five years I've made little effort to do anything and now that I'm beginning to try, everything works for me. I could have hidden from my future for longer. But I am what I am.

Yesterday evening, in an effort to stop myself thinking about Tessa Armstrong, I talked to Mrs Monson again about buying Hope Villa from her. Our negotiations were conducted while watching an old war film on television and drinking whisky. I emphasized the damp, the subsidence, peeling wallpaper, cracked plaster, the need for replumbing and rewiring, the impossibility of her selling to anyone else while the house contained tenants such as myself. She emphasized her love for the house, the number of years she had lived there, her memories of her mother shelling peas and the fact that my room used to be her mother's bedroom.

Her room smelt of rotting apples. One of her friends at the dress factory where she worked gave her apples every year but Mrs Monson never got round to eating them.

The bottle of whisky was nearly empty. Another German bomber plane was being blown up on the flickering black-and-white screen. The armchair where I sat had a greasy cover and worn, dirty arms. I knew Mrs Monson had to sell me the place. It was odd just how certain I was that she would let me have it.

She's not as fond of it as she pretends. When I first arrived she had confessed that her husband, a welder she'd met at a dance hall in Finsbury Park, had never liked Hope Villa. He hated the 'horrid green space' behind it, and slept badly. Most nights, she told me, he had terrible nightmares, usually about the end of the world, and he started to drink heavily soon after moving in. Sometimes, he told her, he saw the world explode in a ball of fire; other nights he saw it all frozen over. But when she talked of moving he would not hear of it. 'It was your parents' house,' he would say. 'You have a responsibility to keep it.'

But Mr Monson drank more and more, and cracks appeared in the walls, and the smell of damp and decay began to creep, very slowly, a little more year by year, into the rooms, and she and her husband drew back, deserting more and more of the rooms, leaving behind furniture and packing cases, until they found themselves making do with the makeshift kitchen and dining room. They even slept there, he on a camp bed, she on a sofa.

It was because of the expense of heating the place, they told each other.

Eventually, when he lost his job after not turning up too many times, they decided to take in lodgers in the empty rooms. Lonely men came and went for some years, filling the spaces with their own memories, leaving behind a few beer cans, empty coffee tins, a mood of despair.

One summer Mr Monson went down to visit Mrs Monson's sister and husband in Hastings while Mrs Monson stayed behind to mind the house.

A few days after he had left, the day before he was supposed to be returning, she read in a newspaper of the accidental drowning of an Islington man. This was before the policeman called round to tell her that the man was her husband.

He was an excellent swimmer and she assumed that he must have gone swimming when drunk.

She was upset, of course, and lonely, but then she had always been lonely, she said.

'Poor Mrs Monson,' I said, the day she confided all this. 'Come to the pub at once.'

I suppose at first I had quite enjoyed Hope Villa, and treated it as I treated most of my life, like a funeral ceremony I was trying hard not to laugh at. Mr Phillips and the twins are so humourless. Mr Phillips never smiles, and resembles an unhappy dinosaur because of his long neck, drooping shoulders and his air of obsolescence. As for the twins, they're even serious about dedicating themselves to pleasure; they have rows of books about sex on their bookshelves which contain ugly pictures of naked, unsmiling people who all look as though they are trying to have a shit.

The twins seem to do nothing but practise at sex, go to meetings on nuclear disarmament and listen to loud music. They hardly ever go to their college, where they are supposed to be students.

Jerry is short, and frowns. Mary is an inch or two taller, and smiles.

'No,' Jerry would say to poor Mrs Monson, 'we haven't the money this week.'

'I'm afraid we haven't the money this week,' continues Mary.

Although Mary has spots, her face always looks clean, a little too clean, as though she has just scrubbed it.

'Our grant still hasn't come through...' Jerry would say.

'It's such a nuisance about the grant,' continues Mary.

'Nuisance about the grant,' echoes Jerry.

They have anti-bomb posters on their walls, obscuring the bright sunflower wallpaper which, Mrs Monson explained to me woefully one day, she had chosen herself many years ago, when her husband was alive.

'The nuclear noose is tightening,' one would say.

'There may be no tomorrow,' announces the other.

'No tomorrows,' echoes the first.

Both would tilt their heads to one side as though they were already victims of some future war, which in a way they probably were.

They wear sensible lace-up shoes, anoraks and trousers – prepared for camping out in a nuclear wasteland.

'Well, I don't know,' Mrs Monson said to me one day. 'I think the worst part of this nuclear-war business is the fear of it.'

'I doubt that,' I replied.

About six months ago I started a bonfire in the tiny scragheap of a garden to burn some of her rubbish.

I stood watching the bonfire for hours, and afterwards Mrs Monson said I looked different.

My face had been red from the heat and I smelt of fire, but it wasn't just that, she said.

My eyes were brighter than before, and even merrier, she said.

A month or so later, although it was summer, I made a fire in the fireplace of the front room which had once been Mrs Monson's parents' best room, but was now unused except by old wrapping paper, packing cases, and the paraffin cans for her heater.

It is a beautiful room, with fine cornices, and it looked much, much better with a fire.

'Lovely,' Mrs Monson had said. 'Something about a real fire.'

'That's right,' I said.

'The only thing is,' she said after a while, 'I don't think we're allowed fires here.'

I brushed my hair back from my forehead.

'I think this is what they call a smokeless zone,' she continued.

I took no notice.

We were silent for a while while we watched, and listened to the crackle of the flames.

'Martin,' she said. 'You'd better put that out. It's against the law.'

I turned round to her, and grinned.

'And what do I care about laws?'

Angrily she shuffled into the kitchen, brought back a jug of water and poured it on to the fire while I watched, still grinning.

'You're a very determined lady, in your way, aren't you, Mrs Monson?'

She said she didn't like my tone, and she left the room.

It wasn't long after this that I started telling her again that the house was going to rack and ruin.

She replied that she was considering selling it, which she wasn't, really, except of course that people always feel like moving in autumn, because they think their unease is due to their house instead of their life's decay.

One evening I mentioned that I might be interested in buying the house.

She had laughed.

'But Martin – you haven't any money.'

I felt my eyes narrow.

'You don't look like a young boy, sometimes, but a dangerous old man,' she said.

At one time I went out every night, often bringing back a different girl.

Sometimes I knew Mrs Monson was standing on the stairs and trying to hear what was going on. Just to see if the girl was all right, she would probably tell herself, listening to the wind against the windows.

It had once been not a grand house but a decent house, Mrs Monson told me one morning angrily. When she was young there had even been a maid in the room next to the twins.

Now that room was unlivable in because the rain seeped in, and even when the weather was hot the room did not dry out.

Her husband had stored his old newspapers in that room. They were still there, sodden masses, a blur of newsprint, but on some the headlines were still visible, excited banners about long-forgotten wars and murders.

But Mrs Monson soon forgave me my bad behaviour, because something about me impresses her. And she likes the fact that I keep a diary because she claims she has a 'great respect for the written word'.

This evening, while talking to Mrs Monson, I was fantasizing about sex with Tessa.

I imagined our lips meeting and her touch sending my mind reeling back and back through time and place (I feel very high-flown about Tessa, although very grubby too).

I would know what she wanted, just as I had always known what she would want.

Our love-making would begin gently (it was admittedly hard to concentrate on the thought of Tessa while sitting next to Mrs Monson's jellified body), in a slow ecstasy of touch and soft murmurings. As it continued it would grow fiercer and fiercer.

Her nails would tear at my back.

My teeth would bite into the soft skin of her neck.

In the half-light of the darkening room (my room) our white skins would glimmer as we struggled, our limbs forming different equations as we linked and kicked and sprawled, hands pushing and pulling and kneading as though one moment they were trying to pull each other apart and the next to mould the flesh into new shapes.

I would trace the long journey down her thighs finding her feet with their delicate soles and coming to the toes which would respond well to the soft slow sucking pressure of my hungry mouth. Tessa's skin would shiver and undulate as if suffering from continual tremors, each patch of skin alive and boiling underneath with molten material.

As we changed position, as my hand sailed up her tummy to the hills of her breasts, as her legs spread out invitingly, a dark new world waiting to be entered, as her head tipped back and her hair flowed around her, oceans of grey seas, it would seem that our bodies were supplying all kinds of answers and questions.

'But when would we all have to move out?' interrupted Mrs Monson's anxious voice. She breathed whisky into my face.

The vision of Tessa's white body, with her eggshell face like a haughty Renaissance painting, vanished abruptly.

'What?' I said.

'When would we have to move out?' she said.

'I can't answer you that quite yet,' I snapped, and got up.

Mrs Monson looked troubled, fat and old.

Back in my room I decided that this kind of scheming really wasn't all that much fun.

I poured myself a bowl of cornflakes for comfort.

The phrase 'the banality of evil' came into my mind.

I decided to contact the insurers at once to make sure that they would insure Hope Villa for a sizeable sum.

10

Tessa Armstrong

Thursday 7 September

ON THE WAY BACK FROM WORK TODAY THERE WAS A SMELL of rotting leaves everywhere.

The clouds were heavy and low.

It thundered a little while later as I was searching through my mother's bedroom for information about her lover.

I went through her wardrobe, checking every pocket.

'You must let me lead my own life,' my mother had said this morning when I asked her who her lover was. 'You mustn't pry.'

She had been pouring muesli into her bowl from too great a height, and she was aiming it slightly to the left of the centre of the bowl. Everything she does is out of focus.

'Why won't you tell me who it is?' I asked her.

'Tessa, I hope you don't mind my saying so but these last few days I think you've been looking rather… different. Are you well?'

'I should like to know who he is.'

'Your eyes,' she said. 'They're so vivid. Perhaps you should see a doctor. Have you got a boyfriend or something? Is that it?'

Still standing up, she took a large mouthful of muesli, which she buys in quantity from some health shop.

She drinks herbal tea instead of coffee.

'You know you really should eat more,' she said. 'You're far too…' – She leant closer to me, as though having a good look for the first time – 'too… gaunt.' She stood straighter, pleased by her retrieval of this unusual word (she only reads gardening and biology books), and placed another mouthful between her lips. 'Why... don't you... try... some... honey?'

'Is he someone I know?' I asked.

My mother frowned vaguely. 'You know... sometimes I wonder if you get enough sleep,' she said. 'Your eyes... and you wander about in a most eccentric way... the neighbours have remarked on it too. Do you want some tea?'

I shook my head. My mother gazed over my shoulder as though mentally potting seedlings over by the wall behind me.

'Did you want some tea?' she repeated.

'No thank you,' I said.

'You look overtired... Your brother's fiancée... Ann... she told me how odd she thought you were, you know. She said she thought the past troubled you. She suggested you should see a psychiatrist. I didn't say anything to you at the time but...'

'You did, as a matter of fact.'

'Pity he's marrying her... she kept touching my arm... I didn't like the way she kept touching my arm when she spoke to me.'

She yawned.

'Why are some people so *personal* all the time? I do dislike it,' she said.

'Look, my father has only just died. I can't think why...' I said.

She cut a rugged piece of brown bread and put it into the toaster.

'Oh,' she said, 'did you want some?'

'No thanks.'

'Now, what was it you were saying...?'

'I was saying that my father...'

She took the honey out of the cupboard. 'He died five years ago,' she said.

'That's not long,' I snapped.

'Oh... it seems... rather a long time... to me.'

'Why won't you tell me who it is?' I asked.

She tried to focus on me again, but lost the battle, and gazed dreamily at the clock.

She sighed.

'I'm staying in tonight though,' she said. 'But I'll be back late from school.'

'Why aren't you seeing him? Is he working? What does he do?'

She smiled to herself, and turned on the radio.

She was wearing a new dress, a black-and-white checked one, which gave her the appearance of a demented chess board.

'He and I are having lunch together actually,' she said.

She poured some apple juice into her glass.

She frowned.

'This is the wrong apple juice. It has additives.'

'I had assumed your lover was already married – that that was why you were so secretive.'

'Sorry?'

'Are you really planning on getting married?'

'I just can't stand this with additives. You know how bad they are for us.'

'Could you try very hard to answer my question? Are you or are you not getting married?'

She stood up. Her eyes were restless.

'To whom?' I said.

She stretched.

'We'll talk about it… later,' she said, and drifted out of the room.

Tonight with pleasure I searched through my mother's clothes, observing that she is not quite so calm as she seems. She has an unreasonable collection of clothes. They suggest moments of frivolity in West End shops: pastel shift dresses, garish skirts I'd never seen her wear, a cowboy-style shirt, a sequinned top. She used to wear simple clothes, because there was only my father to consider, and he clearly had not mattered. Her fingers were always dirty. Out in the garden she had worn her Liberty scarf, wellington boots and vast overcoat. Her gloved hands tugged out sycamore seedling after sycamore seedling and tossed them into the steel barrow. She used to have a steadiness about her, a distance from the flotsam and jetsam of life. But now she jumps when the telephone rings.

She used to live very happily in her private world, a good deal more interested in plants than she was in her husband or indeed any human being.

The bedroom was dark, because of the rain, but I didn't put on the light in case my mother returned and saw it on from out in the street.

The noise of the thunder ripped through the air, as though the sky were being torn up in a rage.

The rain was hitting the windows hard, and I became increasingly involved in this room with its smell of powder and perfume.

I sat at her dressing table and painted my lips with her pink lipstick and my eyelids with her green liquid. I dusted my face with powder flecked with gold so that my skin shimmered in the darkening mirror into which I smiled.

Through the looking-glass the room looked better. Somehow it toned down the pink walls. The new flowery curtains and the matching frill round the dressing table were almost pleasant now.

I knew they came here together sometimes when I was out at work. I'd find the bed disordered, or a meal left half-eaten downstairs, and on occasion I would sense that he had been in my room too, stroking my sheets, touching my clothes. Things were out of place – a sheet rumpled, a cardigan fallen from its hanger, and once a piece of caked mud from a man's shoe.

It amused me to think of him in my room, perhaps without my mother's knowledge, and sometimes I'd leave things out for him to find – a bra, a blouse, something like that.

I picked up a bill from the glass top of the dressing table. It was covered in powder and bits of dust, as though it had lain at the bottom of her handbag for a while. It was from an Italian restaurant just behind the office where I worked. She and he must have been nervous of eating there, I thought, as I held it in my hand. Perhaps they liked the danger. Although of course she would have known how unlikely it was that I would come past, as I never go anywhere, there must have been just a slight fear that I might pass by and look in, perhaps after having forgotten something at the office. One had eaten minestrone, probably her, the other had hors d'oeuvre. Both had eaten liver next. And then one had had a cassata. Probably him. She doesn't like sweet things. Two bottles of wine. Too much. My mother drinks very little, or used to.

I began to file my nails, and after blowing away the nail dust from my fingers, I chose a pearly apricot from the array of varnishes.

I wore only her dressing gown, an old silk gown covered in soft blue patterns and torn at the hem.

It was bought for her by my father on a trip he took to China.

He had bought me a doll on that trip, as he did on every trip. I thought of them up in the attic carefully wrapped in plastic bags, rows and rows of foreign dolls he carried home for his darling daughter he thought was just a child. They used to watch me sternly from my mantelpiece, stout Russian, stately Florentine, exotic Indian. Now they were wrapped up in plastic as if in the mortuary – lifeless, finished with.

He was still calling me his 'little girl' and buying me dolls when I was sleeping with three men a week.

When I had finished my hands, I painted my toe nails.

The thunder was moving closer now. I stood up, stretched and looked out of the window at an elderly woman struggling along with her black umbrella in the wind and the rain.

I keep thinking of Martin Sherman. He doesn't live far from here. He's virtually the boy next door. I keep thinking I'm going to look out and see him standing out in the street looking up at my window. On Saturday I'll see him again.

11

MARTIN SHERMAN

Saturday 9 September

THIS MORNING WHEN I AWOKE I IMAGINED MY ROOM SMELT
of Tessa, her skin, her perfume (in fact it smells of old houses).

I imagined that we had made love last night and afterwards
she had sat on my bed and slowly unplaited her hair, and as she
unplaited it there seemed more and more of it until she sat like
a pre-Raphaelite angel, her pale face and grey hair flooding the
room like moonlight.

Such thoughts made a pleasant contrast to the chill of getting
up and running to the bathroom over the lino.

As I lay in the bath I saw her hot, lovely body with its cold
eyes, watching me.

Earlier, I had looked out of the window at the smudged wet
weather of the Fields. It was like some prehistoric land before
time began, the leaves dripping rain, the grass green, the parked
cars and houses retreating into cardboard cut-outs, their colours
phoney, temporary. I saw a woman without a coat hurrying across
the Fields and I wondered where she had come from, what night
she had spent in whose arms. She was wearing a lilac blouse, an
evening blouse.

The bathwater was lukewarm as usual, and there was a
draught from the ill-fitting window.

I raced from bathroom to bedroom, clasping my towel
to me.

I put on my new grey suit, chosen with great care yesterday.

I spent some time adjusting my appearance in the full-length mirror on the back of the wardrobe door.

Of course, I was not without regret. Gone was the little boy. Gone was the truculent adolescent. Life had been easier before, living alone, in limbo, without connections, just passing the days.

I added a handkerchief to my top pocket and took a few deep breaths before stepping out on to the landing in my new role as a charming and talented business person with great expectations.

At the bottom of the stairs looking up, in apron and stiff dress, stood Mrs Monson. Her seaside-postcard face frowned.

'Whatever are you dressed up like that for?' she asked as I trotted down, dapper and delightful in my grey suit.

'I'm off to see a mortgage broker and a flat,' I said.

She continued to frown.

Her hair was looking more dishevelled than usual, and there were bags under her eyes, although her eyes remained as kindly as ever.

'Look, why don't we just stay as we are, Martin? We've all been happy in our way.'

'But Mrs Monson,' I remonstrated, 'you said you wished to sell to me. Wheels have been put into motion. Words have been said. You can't grab them back. Change has to take place.'

'I don't have to sell to you.'

On the first step where I stood, slightly above Mrs Monson, I moved back a little, as though in shock.

'But Mrs Monson, you gave me your word.'

One fat hand was holding on to the banister.

'Yes, but what about the twins – they're only children really – and what about poor Mr Phillips? I've looked after him for years.'

'But they won't be your concern, Mrs Monson, once you no longer own the place.'

She looked puzzled.

'I assure you, Mrs Monson,' I said, putting my hand on hers. 'Everything will be fine. Trust me.'

I sauntered out of the dark hall into the bright sunlight.

In Highbury Fields, as I passed by, I saw a couple in each other's arms on a bench, quaintly in love among the leaves.

The autumn leaves are still on display there, with matching dogs – ochre spaniels and red setters.

It was a cheerful day now that the rain had cleared. There was sun, a blue sky and some wind.

I used to walk along that street looking for Tessa, although then I didn't know her name or face.

As I waited to see the mortgage broker I observed a few other people sitting importantly reading their newspapers and magazines, each the centre of a tiny world. To me, the women I've seen today look like faulty versions of Tessa which had been discarded from the production line and dumped down here on the streets. Their noses were too long, their shoes down at heel, their faces too pink or too pale. They wore clothes inappropriate to their bodies – trousers which emphasized large bottoms, skirts which showed off bad legs, coats clearly made for other people.

Tessa, however, was surely perfect, I recalled. I imagined her kisses and the way they would leave me damaged.

I thought of the way her nails would rip at my back.

I told my mortgage broker about Hope Villa, and informed him that my mother would guarantee the loan (she had agreed on the phone last night). He was impressed at my mother's name. I had not realized quite how well known a politician she is.

He nodded as I spoke, and called me Mr Sherman, so I impressed him too, I suppose.

For so long I've been outside all that – grey-suited men, doors opening and shutting, listless secretaries, phones and metal desks. My mortgage man is so colourless that it wouldn't surprise me to know he has holes in his feet through which his blood pours out. He has fair hair and small spectacles which ride up whenever he screws up his nose, which is whenever he makes any notes or decisions. As if performing some clumsy dance, the men in their costumes hurry along corridors, burst into rooms, dictate letters. If I blew a choreographer's whistle they'd all leap and turn gracefully in the opposite direction.

It seems that these clothes dress me, ready for a charade, as other clothes in a distant past I can hardly remember have seemed equally temporary and absurd, dressing me for other charades.

But perhaps it is just television and dreams which provide me with the vague memories of other times, other places, always looking for Tessa.

For a moment, as I walked into the estate agent's for my appointment, I decided it was all far too ordinary.

The rodent Mr Richardson was advising a tawny-haired woman in a fur coat who was as artificially elegant as a cosmetic saleswoman. The plumper agent, Mr Thomas, was talking to a fresh-faced son and his parents. The parents reminded me of ducks. They flapped their elbows out as they talked, as though about to fly. Their voices and personalities took more than their fair share of the office. The son looked from one to the other as if he'd been so doing all his twenty-odd years. A man and a woman also waiting sat on two chairs beside each other. Both were staring into the distance. Either they didn't know each other or they'd just had a quarrel.

Meanwhile, right at the end of the office, with her back to the noise, sat Tessa, very still.

'Tessa,' snapped Mr Richardson.

I straightened my jacket.

Tessa stood up slowly and then, still with her back to me, she arched her back, raised her arms and gave an enormous yawn and stretched as though she were coming out of a long sleep.

And then she picked up her coat and swept out of the office into the street.

I followed her out.

She was opening the door of a red mini.

'Get in,' she said. 'Although I can't imagine why you want to see this dump.'

She started up the engine with a roar and went speeding off as though she were the only car around.

'Do you have a special dispensation?' I asked.

'What do you mean?'

'From dying... You drive very dangerously... not that I mind.'

She swerved to avoid a pedestrian.

'Afraid, are you?'

'No,' I said honestly. 'As a matter of fact the idea of dying with you by my side quite appeals to me.'

She didn't reply. She was as beautiful as I remembered, with her influenza-pale skin and fine bones, and the great braid of hair.

Her long white hands rested on the steering wheel, hardly touching it, not quite real.

'Have you been driving for long?'

'For years. Since I was twelve. My boyfriends used to let me drive. I never bothered to take my test, though. Nobody's ever asked to see my driving licence. They all assume I must have one.'

She laughed. Again it was that clear, lovely laugh in contrast to the unnerving quality of her appearance. She looked at me with a slow smile.

I was staring back at her, dazzled I suppose.

Without warning, the car darted into a turning to the right.

She drew up with a screech outside a narrow little house in a cobbled street.

'There,' she said. She took a key out of her pocket. 'You're safe.'

'Are you always as fierce as this?' I asked.

'Today I'm angry.'

She leant over to unlock my door and for a moment everything blurred with the smell of her.

I wanted to kiss her neck. I wanted carefully to move her hair to one side and to press my lips into her neck which would smell even more densely of female flesh.

As she drew back her face was flushed.

'Why are you angry?' I asked, more gently now, more tenderly, as though I had just kissed her.

She looked away. 'My mother. I think she's getting married again but she won't discuss it with me.'

'Is she divorced from your father?'

'He died.'

Suddenly she seemed frail and vulnerable, but maybe that was intended. I still don't know how calculated her charm was. Even that leaning over me, well, it might have been considered. And the adorable blush, was that manufactured?

The car seemed very small and Tessa and I very large and very close. Our breath had filled all the air.

'Do you like the man she's marrying?'

'She won't tell me who he is, so I presume I won't... Get out then,' she said. 'I have to get back to the office soon.'

'Aren't you coming in?'

'Do you want me to come with you?' And again there was the element of enticement. She wanted me to ask her to come in. Nothing was allowed to be simple.

'Of course I want you to come in,' I said softly.

I stood behind her as she put the key in the green door. She was slender and slight. I wanted to encircle her with my arms.

The flat smelt of new paint and old wood.

She hurried round it pouring forth a running commentary which went something like this: 'Delightful fully fitted kitchen with every modern convenience including an oven and a view of a road featuring many cars, superbly compact sitting room round about twelve by twelve but looking considerably smaller once furniture is in. Even more compact bathroom with squashed-in lavatory and no ventilation. Two bedrooms too tiny to fit beds into and then of course, out here, you can just see the roof terrace which anywhere else would be called the roof to the kitchen extension. Note the lack of railings, flowers, pavings, anything which might justify the description of this as a roof terrace...'

We were standing in the square sitting room, with its bare wooden boards and white walls. She had stopped talking and was staring in the direction of the backs of some houses. I stood a little way behind her.

It was hot in the flat.

'Why do you do this job?' I asked after a while.

'What job do you do?' she replied.

'Well, I work in a supermarket... Just as a stacker of tins,' I said.

'And why do you do that job?'

She drew a question mark in the dust on the window which looked out on to the 'roof terrace'.

'This place has been on the market for months. They're asking too much. People are so very greedy,' she said.

'Do you live at home?'

She was dressed more smartly than the last time I'd seen her. But she was still very prim – in a grey cashmere sweater which clung to her breasts (she had taken off her coat) and a plain black skirt.

But there was something very knowing, attractively knowing, about her primness, as though it had all been planned out with great care.

She turned. She didn't seem to have any make-up on – except for her lips, which were red.

'Yes. In a dark little house. In Northwood Road. It's a road full of children but our house is cramped and miserable. It's a very serious house. When my mother marries she'll bring someone unserious in.'

A car passed by, over the cobbled street outside. She jumped slightly as though caught up in the stillness of the day and the quiet streets whose inhabitants were working in their offices, somewhere else.

'And my brother's getting married.'

I was even closer to her now. At any moment I expected her to dance away from me, chattering, glancing back at me like some wretched nymph. But instead she remained very still.

'She thinks I'm unstable.' She pushed away a bit of hair from her face.

'Are you close to your brother?' I asked.

'No. He's an astronomer. Sometimes he's like my father used to be – talking about the wonder of things. I like him then.'

As she talked I became increasingly aware of how alone I'd always been. The supermarket was fine but I had no relationship with anyone there – certainly not the moronic girl assistants with their hunched shoulders, down-turned mouths and dreary voices exchanging monotones about make-up and periods and boyfriends. Last week, I recalled, I had lost all concentration when I built such a tall pyramid of special-offer tinned grapefruit slices that it collapsed a few minutes later without anyone touching it. I accused a small boy who had strayed from his mother of pushing it over. The child denied this vehemently but thankfully no one believed him. (He had a runny nose and a malevolent glint.) He left the supermarket in tears of righteous indignation, his mother looking very ashamed of her offspring, her offspring furious at life's injustice.

'They're all making connections,' she said. 'They'll probably have children. Whereas I… I just seem to be nothing at all… just someone standing still and ageing… of my own choice of course, because it's better like that. But still sometimes it seems very sad. I'm always standing in empty houses or flats looking out at what's going on – down there, for instance, the swings in the back yard, the washing on that line – and it seems that I spend my time in empty houses staring at other people's lives.' She wiped at the dust crossly with her sleeve. 'And sometimes I don't see why I should cut myself off from everything. My brother is going to marry. She's not especially worthy. In many ways she's as bad as I am. Yet she has the hope to marry, and, no doubt, to bring a version of herself into the world and make me into an aunt, even more sterile, more empty, someone else's aunt.'

'I don't see you as anyone's aunt,' I said clumsily.

'I should like to be ordinary. I have tried to be ordinary. At work I at first tried to pretend to be jolly and get sandwiches for everyone. I kept my charm locked up and just presented a pleasant, rather plain person to them all – skinny, pale, like some species of monkey hopping around the place offering them coffee out of polystyrene cups and sandwiches out of paper bags.

'The amiable man who used to run the office – Sam Edwards – accepted my pretence. I suppose that's what being amiable is all about. But sometimes I'd catch him looking at me in a puzzled way out of the corner of his eye.'

She rubbed at the window with her sleeve.

'I never had any personal phone calls, never went out with anyone for lunch, never appeared to make any connections. Which is exactly what I intended. I thought I wanted to remain alone, keeping up a jolly appearance so nobody pried or pitied me or in any way tried to enter my life. But the past keeps dragging me back. It stops me being free. I think a great deal… of the man… who was responsible for my father's death.

'And now I find that everyone around me is forging allegiances, leaving me even more isolated, and I find that I don't want to be that isolated. Do you see?'

I nodded, although she wasn't looking in my direction now but towards the back of a house where an elderly man was busy laying out some underpants on the railings of his balcony. In the next-door house, clearly a gentrified one, the balcony was covered in pots of flowers.

'Everyone spends their time digging themselves in, staking out their patch of land – look at them all.'

I could only see the old man, but I nodded all the same.

'I wish my mother had had some respect for my father, and would remain unmarried. He was a good man. He doesn't deserve her to go rushing off into the arms of the first man who asks her.'

'How did your father die?'

'In a sort of fight… I try not to think about it.'

'Have you told your mother how you feel about her marrying again?'

'She knows how I feel but I'll tell her again, maybe tonight. I want to know who the man is. I want to know why she's being so secretive. I'm sorry to talk so much but I haven't talked to anyone for a long time and I need to talk now. I have always taken what I needed when I needed it.'

She turned round.

'You know, I have avoided men for a long time. In fact, as I say, I have avoided all relationships. I did not want to be part of it all. Not because I despised it but rather because I respected it…' She looked up, and my lips drowned in her lips and my eyes drowned in hers.

'Who are you?' she said.

'Martin Sherman,' I said stupidly.

'Mr Richardson said we look alike, that we could be brother and sister. It was unusually perspicacious of him.'

She was watching me.

Her hands were fluttering by her side.

Her pale pointed face reminded me of a painting in an old children's book of mine of an imp emerging from a cave. I had loved that painting. It was odd how the whole of my past life now seemed strewn with clues about her arrival.

The faint autumn sun was filling the narrow hall where we stood. Everywhere in Islington now leaves lay on paths with their black skeletons showing.

My first girlfriend, Matilda, had something of her arrogance.

My first lover, Anna, had a slim, child's body like hers.

Even the sedate way she spoke had much to recommend her. It reminded me of Carroll's Alice, whom at the ages of eight and nine I admired for her formality and sense of order among the Mad Hatter and Cheshire Cat.

She was talking to me as though she'd been talking to me all her life without knowing it.

It was the sense of recognition, I suppose, which surprised me most of all.

I asked her a few questions about her background just to make sure we really hadn't met before, at some school dance some evening in early youth.

And of course she too was puzzled.

'I never confide in anyone,' she said. 'But I want to tell you everything. I think that's perhaps rather dangerous. Do you think that's dangerous?'

'Not at all,' I said.

'I wish I had met you at a school dance,' she said. 'Where did you live as a child?'

'Epsom,' I said.

'Well, Epsom wasn't that far away. It might have happened. I used to go to Epsom sometimes because my grandparents lived there – my father's parents. We used to eat meringues and play cards. It was very boring. But school dances weren't boring at all.'

'My uniform was grey with a green band round my blazer.'

'I'm sure that would have delighted me,' she said.

'I doubt it,' I replied. 'I imagine you at fifteen rather more concerned with men on motorbikes.'

Her head tilted slightly.

'But I hadn't met you and that green band round your blazer,' she said.

'I'm glad we've met now. It seems an appropriate time to meet.'

The sun lay in panels on the wooden floor.

'Oh I don't know – what were you like at fifteen?' she said.

'Clever – top of the form. Good at Greek, Latin, English. Even good at sports when I bothered. Do you think I'm boasting?'

'I'd believe anything you said that I wanted to believe and I believe all this.'

'I had red hair and freckles as I do now. In photographs I always have a huge grin but my grin doesn't light up my eyes which look calculating and distant. In very early photographs I stand very straight, and look likeable, but as the years go by I lounge more and more until I turn into the person I am now.'

'You don't think you're likeable?'

I grinned. 'Not very.'

'You don't behave as though you've suffered from unpopularity.'

'Popularity and likeableness are by no means the same thing. Besides, I've never wanted to be popular. It has never been an aim of mine.'

'What aims do you have?'

I took her hands. They were warm and soft.

We stood looking at each other.

We were smiling, I recall, and I felt completely happy.

Tessa had grown more beautiful as the time passed. Her face looked fuller, and had lost some of its gauntness. Her cheeks caught a little pinkness from somewhere, not enough to change the quality of her white silk skin but enough to give it a little warmth, as though light were falling onto it from somewhere.

'I like the colour of your hair,' I said. 'I wouldn't have thought I would.'

She looked down, as though shy.

I put my other hand on her hair so that I was holding her head. Even her hair was hot, perhaps from the sun which was shining from behind.

I tilted her face up and I saw she wasn't bashful but sultry and inviting.

She folded herself into my body and my arms were around her and she was young and vulnerable again, and I felt powerful, and kissed her lovely upturned face, which was for a moment empty of all cunning and scorn.

She put her head to one side.

As I leant down to kiss her I thought how odd it was that neither of us had thought to open the door which led out on to the roof, although it was a sunny day.

We both belonged inside.

Her kiss was far warmer than I imagined, very moist and personal and shocking.

We didn't touch except with our mouths. Our hands dropped to our sides.

When her kiss let me go it left me empty inside, as though I had just seen some moving scene of human tragedy.

I suppose I was looking at her with startled eyes.

She smiled and brushed my cheek with her hand, like an accomplished courtesan with a young lover. I couldn't imagine why I had earlier thought her innocent.

I could hear the cars in the distance, turning into streets, coming out of them, people busily pretending their lives were important, whereas it seemed that Tessa and I were among the few who tried to make our lives unimportant.

'Do you remember your first kiss?' I asked.

'Oh yes – I remember my first kiss,' she replied.

'Mine was very chaste. It was in a field in Dorset when I was on holiday with my parents.'

'Was it nice?'

'Oh yes.'

'Did you break her heart?' she asked.

'Yes – I think I did. I've never been... very kind, you see. I think I should warn you of that. Kindness has never been part of my nature. She called on my house once, years later, and she was quite lovely. So it has perhaps been a mistake not to reply to her many letters. It was just... that they were very silly letters.'

'Yes,' she said, touching my face with her hand. 'You do sound unkind... and what do you intend to do to me? Are you going to break my heart?'

'That would be difficult.'

'Oh it might snap easily.'

I kissed her soft lips again.

They melted into mine as though she needed my lips as much as I needed hers.

She tried to pull away.

'I should get back to the office.'

'Nonsense. You should never go back to that office.'

She laughed.

'What do you mean?'

'You shouldn't go back, that's all.'

'How arrogant you are.'

She didn't return to her office but came back with me to Hope Villa, and we made love, tenderly at first, here on the crumpled bed.

Afterwards she said everything was much clearer to her. She said she even knew who her mother's lover was.

She's gone now but she has left behind the stain of her lipstick on my pillow and scratch marks all down my back.

12

TESSA ARMSTRONG

Sunday 10 September

I WAS STANDING AT THE TOP OF THE STAIRS WHEN MY MOTHER came through the door early this morning.

She hummed to herself as she hung up her voluminous coat, one of the few remnants of her former talent for shabby dressing.

She caught sight of herself in the hall mirror, and pursed her pink lips, while patting her hair which was escaping from its large bun. There were shadows of middle age under her eyes and running down from her nose. She frowned, and turned away from her reflection.

She wore a white blouse with a pie-frill neck, as though her head were to be served at some potentate's dinner table. The blouse was tucked into a full tartan skirt.

She looked pretty enough, because she is a beautiful woman with peace about her features, generated mostly by her lack of interest in anything. But her face did not go well with the blouse, and the blouse did not go well with the skirt, and the skirt did not suit her high-heeled shoes, and it was all too girlish for someone whose attraction is a certain mature beauty.

There is something radiantly healthy about my mother and her forget-me-not blue eyes, as though she ought to be hiking over the Austrian alps in search of periwinkles instead of holed up in a dark mausoleum of a school and a house with only a patch of garden at the back.

I began to walk down the stairs.

'Oh Tessa!' said my mother. 'I didn't see you there.' Her face darkened slightly. Her eyes lost their clarity for a moment. She brushed some strands of hair from her face as though trying to brush away the shadow my presence always cast over her.

'I know who it is,' I said when I was about four steps above my mother, looking down. 'I've guessed.'

My mother was frowning up at me.

'I said I know who it is,' I said again. 'It was really very obvious.'

'What on earth are you talking about?' said my mother, in a gusty voice, and swept into the kitchen. She switched on the radio.

She fumbled with the tuner for a while (she was not good with mechanical things).

I stood at the doorway, a severe, watchful figure.

A clear voice rang out '... Only say that you'll be mine... no other arms entwine...'

'I've guessed. I don't know how I could have been so stupid and not realized before. But everything seems much clearer now,' I said.

My mother busied herself around the kitchen – watering her plant, washing up a few cups left out, putting things away.

'You heard what I said,' I announced. 'Why him? Of all people, why him?'

My mother was staring out into her little garden.

'I miss our old garden,' she said.

'I can see him so clearly in my mind. That awful expression of self-satisfaction,' I said. 'His blond curly hair he keeps long. His attempts to be slightly outlandish, not to be one of the crowd. He used to wear velvet suits – but now he just wears clothes that are just a bit different, doesn't he? I'm right, aren't I? He's fatter than he was... But still, he is charming, no one could deny that he's charming, and I suppose you are easily charmed. His voice is so nice, isn't it? So gentle after my father's great booming foghorn. You have to lean closer in order to hear him because his voice is so soft, and some of the things he says are quite tender, because it is easy to say tender things. He often takes your hand, doesn't he? And his skin is very warm, and soft, like a woman's. I bet he talks about my father a lot. I bet he's obsessed by my father. That's right, isn't it? Or perhaps you haven't noticed…'

My mother was still gazing out at the garden; watching the grey and rainy air in between the branches of the trees.

'Is he still married?' I asked.

'No – he's divorced now.'

'But I expect he still has girlfriends too,' I said. 'Only you'd choose not to notice that of course.'

Soft rain was falling, blurring the scene outside.

'And the terrible thing about him is that actually, behind all the posturing and the vanity, there was quite a serious person. Sometimes when I was with him I could see that person, a small, serious, northern little boy with glasses and ambition. And it's that which makes him lovable now, that sense of loss which hovers about everything he does, as though he knew something once which he no longer knows now.'

'He's very well educated,' said my mother in a dead voice. 'He studied history at Cambridge, and he got a First.'

'I know Alexander Bartley got a First. He told me so himself,' I said.

'I wish you'd leave me alone, Tessa. I really do wish you'd leave me alone.'

'Did you ever love my father? Or did you love Alexander all along?'

'Of course not.'

'This morning I've been up in my room thinking, interpreting the past in the light of this new realization about you and Alexander. And I want very much to know: did you have an affair with him before my father died?'

'No, of course not.'

'I seem to remember that you watched him all the time. I didn't think anything of it then. But now...'

'We met again last year. He phoned up here. I don't know why you're so suspicious. It really is quite ridiculous.'

'You're speaking the truth, are you?'

'Of course I am,' said my mother.

'You know, you shouldn't be having an affair with your husband's killer,' I said, 'and you most certainly shouldn't marry him.'

I turned and left the room.

I called Martin. He's coming to collect my things. I'm moving in with him. I don't want to stay in this house any more. I don't want to stay in this house where my mother and my father's killer have made love amongst my father's possessions.

I have just been up to the attic and taken down a suitcase which contains my father's old diaries and letters. She doesn't deserve them.

They smell of damp and decay like my collection of dolls which lay beside the old suitcase wrapped in plastic. But in spite of their wrappings the dolls have been eaten by mice or rats. The Russian one has lost an arm and the Florentine one has been disembowelled. The beautiful costumes are in tatters. And they were such lovely dolls.

PART II

13

ALEXANDER HAD BEEN SURPRISED WHEN MARIAN CALLED late that Sunday morning, just a few hours after leaving his flat, and suggested they meet for lunch.

However, the thought of a large plate of spaghetti (Alexander was greedy) had appealed to him, although he found the particular restaurant's high concentration of the under-fives for Sunday lunch somewhat unsettling.

He was ten minutes late.

From the moment he saw Marian's face he knew what had happened. She was suddenly thin, a different person from the well-mattressed, calm woman who had left his flat just that morning. He prided himself on her calmness – considering it a tribute to his sexual technique. This shaky individual was not the one he knew, who helped to support his self-respect by her continual admiration and air of wonderment at his wit and attainments.

This woman had shadows under her eyes and a jerky way of tearing her bread up into small morsels.

'She knows about us – about our engagement,' said Marian. 'I know she had to some time but she frightens me. She's so... malevolent. I don't know why she should hate you so much. You were tried and acquitted. It was just an accident.'

She was sitting with her back to the French windows.

Behind her, in the garden, a slight breeze stirred the leaves on the trees. Marian talked on.

A toddler stumbled by wearing a navy velvet dress with a lace collar, with the serious expression of an elderly choirboy. The little girl pressed her nose against the window.

'And then – her boyfriend came round. She'd phoned him.'

'Her boyfriend?'

She nodded, blinking a little nervously. How large her hands are, thought Alexander as she picked the bread apart.

'His name's Martin Sherman. He's got red hair and strikes me as rather, well, unconventional. He lives in Baalbec Road, just round the corner, in a house called Hope Villa. He tried to be polite, but there was something about him – he didn't seem at all polite.'

'And why did he come round?'

'He came to collect her things.'

'What?'

'She's moved out. To live with him. Tessa said she was going to see you and tell you what she thought of you. I said she mustn't, you had heart trouble – and anyway I wouldn't tell her where you lived.'

The big airy restaurant, with its tiled floor and white walls, suddenly seemed very cramped to Alexander and he could hardly breathe.

'To live with him? At her age?'

He took a gulp of wine.

'She's twenty,' said Marian. 'That's hardly young.'

'It's disgusting. Besides, she's too unstable still. You've said so yourself on a number of occasions. She shouldn't be allowed to run off with the first young man she meets.'

'She was angry. She took a suitcase containing Tom's old letters and diaries too, from the attic.'

'You didn't tell me about this boyfriend. You should have told me. I have a right to know.'

'She's only just met him. He works in a supermarket.'

'What's his name?'

'I told you. Martin Sherman. He seemed very taken with her – couldn't keep his eyes off her.'

Alexander sat back in his seat.

He grabbed at a packet of grissini, tore it open, and cracked the breadsticks into small portions. He plunged one small portion into the butter, looked at it, then put it down.

Alexander pushed away the spaghetti which was placed before him.

'I should go round there, to his house, and have a word with her,' he said. 'Martin Sherman, Hope Villa, Baalbec Road.'

'Now?' Mrs Armstrong blinked at him.

'Right now.'

'Darling – do stay and finish your food.'

'No thanks,' he snapped, pushing it a little further away.

'But darling, why must you see her? It won't do any good. It's been years since you saw her. She hardly knows you. She probably won't even recognize you.'

He stared at the tapeworm mass of pasta.

'I have responsibilities... I'm going to be her father,' he murmured.

'Don't be ridiculous. You have no responsibilities towards her. No one has. She's on her own. She always has been.'

A waiter ground pepper over the spaghetti.

'Poor child,' said Alexander.

'Tessa was never a child,' said Mrs Armstrong.

'Sometimes, Marian,' said Alexander, 'you can be very uncaring.'

He stood up, and left the restaurant.

14

IT WAS A CLOSE DAY, WARM FOR THIS TIME OF YEAR, TOO warm, Alexander thought as he drove towards Martin's house down Highgate Hill. He saw London laid out below him, an enchanted city made of grey turrets and steeples.

Earlier that morning, he had gone for a walk and passed houses and plants and trees which all looked like exhibits encased in the hot still air.

The laurel leaves had been dusty and a red rose reared up above him looking very lush and dense and faintly threatening.

A young man wearing earphones lurched by him. He suddenly sung out 'The moon is bloody' in a discordant voice.

Sunday morning used to be a family time for Alexander when he played with his two small children, but now it was a solitary period. It was odd, he thought as he walked that morning, how dislocated everyone was from everyone else. He hadn't noticed before that the joggers, the people wearing earphones, everyone was involved in solitary action.

As he drove towards Tessa's house he knew he should have kept away from Tom's memory, and from Tessa.

He should not allow himself this other secret and compulsive existence.

Alexander parked the car in Highbury Place.

He had difficulty getting his breath so he went for a short walk on Highbury Fields to calm himself.

Before he had met Tessa he had had no problems with his

health. Everything had been so much easier then: his affairs, his charm, his success at work.

The big tent of a circus stood way down the end. He could hear music coming from that direction.

It looked a long way off, and rather splendid, well lit by sunshine.

He used to come here with his children on Saturdays to visit one of his colleagues.

He had come once with just his daughter Rebecca and they'd gone to the circus, and she had fallen between the seats and had dropped her popcorn. It had been one of those absurd circuses with no animals but she had still sat enraptured – hand over her mouth when the trapeze artist climbed, finger pointing in amazement when the trapeze artist swung. Afterwards, along with the other children, she had tried climbing with no success the ropes which kept the tent up.

A few people – robustly youthful men and women – were playing tennis. Some loutish lads were showing off some excellent football elsewhere in the Fields. He watched for a while. But his heart wouldn't stop thumping.

His friend Max who lived in one of the Georgian houses which flanked Highbury Fields had told him all about the area, which had all been dairy farms except for a few secluded villas and the terraces of gentlemen and successful merchants. The only bit of high living had been at the riotous Highbury Barn, a pleasure house which indulged in such wickedness as French dancing, to the outrage of local inhabitants. In the 1850s it was proposed that all this area should be turned into a 300-acre park as this was one of the highest locations in the suburbs (hence its name) and known for the sweetness of its air. Plus it was within only two miles of the City. But of course that never happened and all the people from the area crammed for recreation into this odd, rather lovely little park encircled by its majestic houses dreaming of the past.

He wondered if he would visit his friend today – before he visited Tessa.

If he called on Max he would be welcomed in, given drink, conversation. He could be mischievous, devastating Alexander Bartley chuckling about office gossip – all glee and good humour. The other Alexander Bartley who was here now, standing in the street, outside things, a man with hunched shoulders and secret longings, would no longer exist.

Although of course he would have to put up with Max's wife's disapproval. She had made it clear she thought little of the way he had walked out on his wife and children (this was ridiculous of course: he had provided his wife with a handsome settlement, and the children were fine – a bit quiet, but otherwise fine).

Besides, he was not sure that he wanted to relinquish this mood of his. At least it felt real, whereas the rest of his life was increasingly insubstantial.

For the last few years Alexander's real life had been as a shadowy figure sitting in the middle of a dingy cinema. On the screen were continuous shots of Tessa, somewhat hazy shots, poorly filmed, sieved through Marian's memory or his own. But he didn't mind about the quality. He just sat there, open-mouthed, as the days went by.

And all the time he had known, as he knew now, that he should not try to approach the girl on the screen.

Furtiveness, which had always been a part of Alexander's character, and the main reason why he used to indulge in so many affairs, he knew had now solidified into his second self. This self hurried along dark streets with collar turned up, peered through keyholes, fantasized; while the self that everyone saw was as good-looking, as welcoming, as insincere and beguiling as ever.

Alexander had visited Tessa's house many times.

Last week, when Mrs Armstrong went down to the shops and left him alone in the house, he had drawn back the covers of

Tessa's bed and felt and smelt the sheets where she had lain. He opened her wardrobe door, too, and touched each of her dresses and her skirts, one by one, fingering their material in a kind of shy ecstasy. Right at the back of the wardrobe, hanging from a hook behind the other clothes, was the purple silk dress she had worn for him the night her father died.

He remembered how soft and fragile she had felt wearing that as he had held her in his arms, a silk bird, a hummingbird.

Her room was small and dark and very neat, as though she had tried to tidy all her magic away in drawers, in wardrobes, in the little desk by the window. But the room was still strange, full of an undefinable sense of her, of her kisses, of her nails on his flesh, of the blackness in her eyes and in her soul.

There was a photograph of her father on her desk, tall, smiling, receiving some award or another.

He hated the way Tom watched him even here, in the privacy of his secret desires.

'Hello, darling, I'm back,' Mrs Armstrong had shouted.

He had stood on the landing, shaking.

'Come up here,' he said. 'Come up here, darling. Come to bed.'

Alexander was baggier now than he had been five years ago, when he fell in love with Tessa. In those days, he had what he thought of as an angelic face, but nowadays he had more of a – well, cherub's face. It was paler too, and he had lines splaying out from his eyes: fairly charming lines, chuckle lines, because even nowadays Alexander often hunched up his shoulders and produced that slightly sly but good-humoured chuckle which made other people laugh uncomfortably with him. He was still quite popular, in spite of what had happened, but nobody trusted him. They thought him charming, well-informed, a good conversationalist and at times a first-class journalist, but there was something about him, a certain odour of death, which prevented anyone getting close to him.

He walked back towards Baalbec Road; the houses there were ugly red-brick Victorian buildings, a contrast to the elegant Georgian structures.

He kept thinking of that smile of hers.

Some days he thought it was like going into a sweet shop as a child and being told you could have whatever you liked.

Other days he remembered it as an executioner's smile.

But mostly he just remembered the effect it had had on him, the way at the moment of her first smile the whole of his surroundings had been sent spinning away. The trees, flowers, people had gone and all that had been left was that smile, caught forever on that hot summer's day.

The house where she was staying keeled over to one side and had two large cracks in the brickwork. The windows were filthy and the paint was flaking off everywhere. He couldn't even make out the colour of the door. He thought it had probably once been a shade of yellow.

He pressed the bell. He didn't hear it ring. He waited a minute. He could hear his heart pumping away. He straightened his coat lapels. He tidied his hair. He made sure his tie was properly done up. He observed with distress that his blue suede shoes were slightly scuffed.

He tried to present a charming, roguish face.

Eventually a voice shouted out, 'Who is it?'

'My name's Alexander Bartley... does Martin Sherman... live here?'

The door opened on the chain and he saw a woman's big face.

'Yes,' she said abruptly.

'Could I possibly – have a word with the young lady,' he asked. 'I'm... well actually I'm going to be the father of the young lady.' He paused, aware that his words sounded odd. 'She is here, isn't she? Tessa.'

The woman opened the door cautiously. She had vast hips

which protruded on either side of her like trays. Her make-up was a few layers thick but beneath it all was a reasonably pleasant face, neither old nor young, but somewhere in a plumpish, ageless period in between.

Her hands were small and fat.

'Come in then. I'll call them.'

The hall had black-and-white diamond tiles on the floor, giving it the air of a public lavatory. The plastic lampshade was blistered in places, and swung in the draught.

He could see the dust hanging in the air.

She turned and yelled, 'Martin!' at the top of her voice. 'Is that girl still with you? There's a man to see her. Says he's going to be her father.'

The woman glanced at Alexander again, severely.

Although the house overlooked Highbury Fields at the back, it didn't seem to be affected by the green grass and the stretching trees. The house was turned in on itself.

A tall gawky man drifted anxiously, like a piece of dust, across the landing.

'Not for you, Mr Phillips, dear, for Martin,' she said.

The man called Mr Phillips nodded and vanished.

Eventually a red-haired boy appeared at the top of the stairs.

'Who wants me?'

'This gentleman here,' said Mrs Monson. The woman stood differently at the sight of Martin, with a slight simpering movement of the hips.

'Thank you...' said Alexander.

'Mrs Monson's the name,' she said, and pottered off down the hall.

The boy's hair was ruffled and his clothes had not quite settled on him, as though he'd only just tugged them on.

Alexander decided he had been making love to Tessa and felt angry and indignant.

'Excuse me,' said Alexander, 'but I've come to get Tessa.'

'I'm sorry?' said the boy, who had a far posher accent than his untidy appearance would have suggested.

'Tessa. I want Tessa. She really must come home at once. She can't go wandering off like this.'

'And who exactly are you?' the boy asked.

'Alexander. My name is Alexander Bartley. I'm going to be her father. Well… I'm going to marry her mother.'

The boy nodded, and began to walk down the stairs towards Alexander.

He had an impudent look about him, and in spite of the grace with which he moved, the scattering of freckles over his nose, the boyish charm, he struck Alexander as aggressive. His mouth was wide and his eyes were blue and dancing.

He grinned at Alexander.

'I don't think she'd want to see you, Mr Bartley. She's a bit upset, you see, about you and her mother.'

'Well,' protested Alexander, 'I really don't see…'

'She thinks it's outrageous that you intend to marry her mother, in the circumstances. I think she sees it all as rather a betrayal.'

'Well… I'm afraid I don't see that…'

'She thinks you should have kept away from her family… after what happened…'

'I can hardly help it if…'

'She firmly believes it would be better for everyone if you were to give up her mother, right now. She suggests you might like to be posted somewhere abroad, to get over the whole thing.'

'I have no intention…'

The boy shrugged. 'I am only reporting what she said. I personally am making no comment.'

He smiled pleasantly. His eyes had a look which reminded Alexander of the eyes of Tessa.

Two of a kind, thought Alexander, these two are two of a kind.

The boy's belt wasn't properly done up.

Alexander disliked the boy's air of rampant sexuality and his wide lips.

'All the same,' said Alexander, 'I should like to speak to her myself.'

'She's still too upset,' said the boy, shaking his head a little. 'She couldn't possibly see you.'

'I don't hear any weeping,' said Alexander.

'She's a very quiet weeper,' said Martin, barring Alexander's way. Alexander observed that Martin's arms were muscular.

'I don't know whether you are aware of it,' said Alexander politely. 'But Tessa is very fragile. She has been in a very bad psychiatric condition for some years now.'

'Really? Curious then that nobody sent her to see a doctor, don't you think?'

'Her mother thought it best to leave her as she was. She thought Tessa would come out of it all in her own time.'

'Well, she has now, hasn't she?'

The boy smiled again.

'I think the best thing you can do Mr Bartley, is to calm down and leave her be. From what I gather, you've been involved quite enough in her life already.'

Alexander fumbled in his pocket for his cigarettes. 'She's OK, is she?' he said softly.

'Not too bad,' snapped Martin.

Alexander took out his wallet. 'Perhaps you could give her these…' he said, taking out four fifty-pound notes. 'It might be a difficult time,' he murmured.

'She won't want those,' said Martin, 'thanks,' and turned his back on Alexander. Alexander watched him go up the stairs. At the top he turned.

'Goodbye, Mr Bartley,' he said.

'Look… I do care about her, that's all. I'm concerned about her welfare. Tell her that, would you?'

'I'll tell her,' said the boy.

He grinned again. It was a curiously empty grin, and yet full of life at the same time.

He looked down at Alexander as if from a great height.

Later that night, as Alexander lay in bed with Marian he couldn't get that red-haired, derisive figure out of his mind.

15

WHEN ALEXANDER PHONED TESSA THE FOLLOWING MORN-
ing, to his astonishment she agreed to meet him. 'I would have seen
you yesterday,' she said, 'but Martin wouldn't let me. We need to
have… a little talk about your marriage. I think you should know
my views. Before it's too late.'

'Quite,' said Alexander. 'That's exactly what I think. I should like
to have a proper discussion. Have it all out. When can I see you?'

His secretary watched him thoughtfully, as he dragged at his
cigarette.

'Look,' he said, 'why don't we meet for a drink? That would
be the civilized thing to do, surely?'

He could feel his skin very hot and uncomfortable. He kept
swallowing.

'Do you think that would be sensible?' said Tessa.

'Why yes, I'm sure it would. Quite certain it would be.' His
hand holding his cigarette was trembling. 'Yes. We'll meet tonight
at the Club, in Greek Street. At about seven. That's if your fierce
boyfriend will let you out… And please don't ask if he could come
too. This is really just something we two have to talk about.'

'Well all right, seven tonight then.'

'Are you OK?' said Alexander's secretary Helen, with whom
he had had an intermittent affair for many years. 'You look pale.'

'Fine,' he said. 'Absolutely fine.'

He stubbed out his cigarette. He coughed. He lit another. She
made him a cup of coffee.

'Could you cancel my early evening appointment?' he said. 'Something more urgent has come up.'

He stared for an hour at an article about rail strikes, and ended up crossing out just half a paragraph.

'You know, Alexander, sometimes you try to do too much,' said his secretary.

'Too much work?'

'No – you try to fit too much into your life. Too much fun. Too much excitement. You can't have it all.'

He frowned at her. 'And you? You do the same,' he said.

'I'm not talking about you and me – you know that. It's just that I care about you. A lot of people care about you. You dance too close to the edge.'

He smiled, that smug smile of someone who thinks he can get away with anything.

'Try to behave yourself,' she said.

'Are you jealous, darling? I can't believe you're jealous.'

'Oh – I gave up being jealous long ago,' she said.

Just before seven Alexander left work and walked over to the Club.

It was drizzling, and every now and again a gusty wind threw rain in his face.

He thought of Tessa's lovely auburn hair, now grey. He remembered the austerity he had seen in her face when he had entered her office last week. Was it last week? He was losing track of time. Her grey hair, all his fault. He liked the fact that it was all his fault. He liked the idea of having affected her in the past, and of affecting her in the present without her being aware that he was doing so. He enjoyed the knowledge that he had chosen her mother's new car in which she sometimes sat, that he had bought the television she sometimes watched, that Mrs Armstrong followed his advice about the handling of Tessa – to leave her be, not to send her to a doctor, not to buy her new clothes.

And now he was coming towards her again, through grey streets.

He walked into the dark hallway of the Club and left his coat with the girl there, who greeted him respectfully by name.

He ran his fingers through his hair, which was curly and a little fluffy from the rain.

At first he couldn't see her.

There was so much movement, and for a moment he felt lost and young, like that other self which had existed before he had discovered he could do most things better than other people.

'Hello Alexander,' called a voice from the bar. The voice's owner wore a mustard-yellow jacket and a dislocated expression.

Alexander nodded, but had no idea who the mustard-yellow man was.

'Hi,' said Alexander.

Someone else grabbed at his sleeve.

'Oh Alexander – I'd been meaning to ask you about an article…'

'Terrific,' said Alexander after a while. 'Send it along.'

He had seen Tessa at the far end of the room.

He knew she had seen him too, although she didn't show it.

And then their eyes met, and she smiled, and her eyes were for a moment as though seeing an old friend after a period of absence.

But almost at once the shutters closed down and she was again that figure of desire and reproach.

He came towards her.

His stomach was fluttering like a teenager's – full of escaped fears, bats and butterflies – as he drew closer to Tessa.

Her head was to one side, and she now wore a wry sort of smile.

Her eyes were heavily made-up, almost disappearing in the darkness of the surrounding kohl.

'Well,' said Alexander.

'Well, well, well,' said Tessa, her head to one side.

She laughed.

She offered him her hand, as though this were all just fun, an entertainment, quite unserious.

'You look as beautiful as ever,' he said gallantly.

'I was telling Tessa,' said a girl sitting next to Tessa as Alexander dropped into the seat beside them, 'how surprised I was to see her here, of all places.' The girl laughed, a false kind of grating laugh. 'This is the kind of place one progresses to, not arrives at the moment one decides to, as it were.'

'This is Nicola,' said Tessa. 'An old acquaintance of mine. She hasn't left me alone since I came in here.'

'Alexander and I know each other,' said Nicola.

Alexander gave the girl a second look and recalled a drunken evening a year or so ago.

'I hope you didn't mind my ordering,' Tessa said as the waitress poured out some champagne. 'But I was thirsty.'

He watched Tessa with puzzlement. She gave no appearance of a girl who'd been out of the world for five years, who had been only fifteen when she stepped aside. Instead, every movement, every expression, every action had the assurance and sophistication of a woman many years older. She looked around loftily. Gone was that pretence of cute enthusiasm. Now her attraction was cooler and Alexander felt cold, all the way through he was cold.

The piano started up, playing the tunes of old Beatles' songs.

'What a curious place this is,' she said. 'I don't know if I like it very much.'

Her high-necked suede dress had tiny little buttons which ran all the way up, right beneath her chin.

'Oh I like it a lot,' said Nicola. 'I often come here.'

'Really?' said Tessa. Her skin was odd, almost transparent, and her head was tilted in a questioning angle. Her lips were moist from champagne.

'I'm meeting my friend Geoffrey here,' said Nicola. 'But I'm a bit early, and he's always very late. You know,' she confided to Alexander, 'sometimes he doesn't turn up at all. Wife problems.'

The Club was crowded with good-looking people or famous people (few were both) gesticulating and greeting each other with exaggerated gestures as though they were on stage. The waitresses all had identical long legs and blonde hair and wore little aprons over their short black dresses.

Behind the bar, sleek waiters shook cocktails in silver shakers, and panels of glass reflected the movement.

'I thought you were at university,' said Tessa, 'in Oxford.'

Nicola nodded at someone over the other side of the room. She looked deliberately distant and important.

'To be honest, it's a bit of a child's playpen. It's beautiful of course, and I enjoy the academic work, but well, London has more going for it. Especially from a career point of view. Don't you think, Alexander?'

She turned to Alexander. He nodded. She was sitting close to him, whereas Tessa was on the other side of the round glass table, a long way away, regarding them both with what he knew was amusement. Nicola was a pretty girl, dark, slim and vivacious. Conventionally attractive, full of vitality, all those ordinary phrases. And all the while, watching, was Tessa who transcended time or place. She sat very still. At any moment, with one of her smiles, he thought, she could have the whole room at her command. She could stand up, smile quietly to herself, walk to the bar, and the atmosphere in the club would have changed, would have been stilled, would suddenly become eerie as she caught the souls of the silly, shouting young men and made the self-satisfied television performers and journalists hold on to their hearts as they experienced a sensation of falling, shooting down a lift shaft in a lift with no destination.

It would have been better for everyone, he thought, if Tessa had stayed where she was, in her dark little room, brooding on the past.

Alexander and Tessa watched each other while Nicola chatted. He wanted Tessa very badly. It was all he wanted in the world, all he had ever wanted. Most of all, he just wanted to kiss her. He wanted to put his lips on hers. And he wanted to hold her very close. If he held her very close he felt that all his misery would go away. If he squeezed her tightly enough it would all disappear. His awful sense of distance would go. Inanimate objects and living objects would get their colour back. Everything would come back into place, whereas right now everything was spinning around in a disorderly fashion as though in the control of a naughty almighty poltergeist.

He had been so lonely for so long now.

He wished love would go. He wished someone would take it off him. He wished one could sell it to someone as one could sell unwanted bits of furniture. He wished someone would arrive in a vast van and take this love away. It was blocking up his whole life.

He was no longer the chirpy seducer with luck and talent on his side, an overgrown cupid with intellect.

Nicola waved at someone across the room.

'Tessa's marvellous, isn't she?' she said to Alexander, gaily. 'She can always get the better of anyone. She always could, you know. A remarkable girl. I'd rather be left alone in a pit of tigers than with her.' Nicola laughed again. 'But we used to get along well, in our way. As long as I always played second fiddle. I used to be good at that.' She smiled at Tessa good-naturedly. 'We had quite a good time. Going to clubs.' She looked around. 'Not like this of course, not smart London drinking clubs with restricted membership and good-looking women at the door. No, we used to go to really sleazy places off Oxford Street and pick men up, for the fun of it. Didn't we, Tessa? She was the leader, of course. She decided where we'd go and who we'd pick up and usually what we'd do with them afterwards. We were a pretty pair, you see. Fourteen-year-old pouting bundles of prettiness, weren't we? My parents never knew. They used to leave me alone with Tessa in the house, with my elder brother. But my brother stayed out all night anyway so we could do what we liked. It amused us. We'd play different parts on different evenings. Sometimes Tessa would be sweet and mild and I'd be tough, other times she'd be tough and I'd be sweet. Sometimes we'd be twenty, sometimes we'd be twelve. I suppose it was just one up from dressing-up games. But it was with real people, and it wasn't innocent at all, I wouldn't want you to think it was innocent you know. There wasn't anything innocent about it. And then one night we went too far, and after that we stopped going out together didn't we, Tessa?'

Tessa nodded.

'Life was difficult for me for a long time after that – I felt bad about what had happened – but eventually I came through. At school she never seemed to have a conscience. It was why everyone admired her so much, I think. But then after her father died she changed. She became quite kind. Then she left. I've thought about her a lot, you know, over the years.'

Alexander ordered another bottle of champagne. The eyes of Tessa and Nicola were bright, animals in the night.

The two of them were older than he'd ever been, he thought. He had thought himself so tough, so sophisticated, so wily, and yet compared with these two he was a child, a blue-eyed creature of daytime.

From over the other side his friend Peter Miles the playwright was coming towards them. Alexander wished he hadn't arranged to meet Tessa here. He wondered why he had. He supposed he thought he'd feel safer here, surrounded by people he knew. He had thought it would be easier to play his old role, his charming role.

'So tell me about this boyfriend,' Nicola was saying.

'I've moved in with him,' said Tessa.

'He's the son of Mary Sherman,' said Alexander. 'Your mother tells me.'

'That's right,' said Tessa.

Nicola was silent for a moment.

'The politician?' said Nicola.

'Yes,' said Alexander.

'You would choose the son of the woman who is rapidly becoming the most influential politician in the country,' said Nicola. 'How did you meet him?'

'He just turned up, where I worked.'

'Is he smart like his mother?'

'Very smart.'

Peter Miles had stopped to talk to someone. Alexander realized that even if things were different, if Tessa had loved him, if her father hadn't died, his life would have been miserable from the moment she smiled because he would never have been sure of her. Even now, knowing that Peter, whom women always adored, might come over, he felt a little sick inside with apprehension.

'Have you met her boyfriend, Alexander?' said Nicola.

'Yes. He rather alarmed me.'

'What does he do?'

'He's investing in property,' said Tessa.

'Oh no doubt he'll do well. He wanders into your office. He falls in love with you. He dabbles in property. He's lucky. Meanwhile I expect his mother climbs to new heights of power, leaving the way open for you two to found some family like the Kennedys. You once said that was what you wanted. Is that it?' She laughed again, that empty laugh.

'If you're inquiring whether or not Martin and I will one day get married, the answer is I'm not sure yet. If you're asking whether or not I should like to have children, the answer is that yes, on the whole, I probably would. Life is a pretty hopeless matter without them, I would have thought. If you're asking if I should like to belong to a dynasty like the Kennedys, I have to say that I consider that a rather vulgar and silly question.'

'But is Martin politically ambitious?'

'I think he might consider going into politics, if he were to have sufficient financial stability.'

'She talked like this before, you know,' said Nicola. 'Even when she was a girl she talked like a Victorian. She chose her words well, as if out of a vast vocabulary.'

'Hi,' said the playwright, standing behind Tessa, not seeing Tessa but seeing Nicola, who smiled at him winningly.

Tessa was watching Alexander, as though she guessed his anxieties.

Fortunately, at that moment someone shouted Peter's name and he turned.

'See you,' he said in an unduly intimate voice to Nicola who looked dazed.

'So that's him,' said Nicola after he had wandered off, and Alexander could have sworn that she sighed.

'You stick with Geoffrey,' said Alexander. 'Peter would only break your heart.'

'I am at an age,' said Nicola, 'when one quite wants a broken heart.'

The room was becoming more crowded, and Alexander wished Geoffrey would turn up. He wanted to be alone with Tessa.

'Hi there,' said a voice from nowhere in a phoney American drawl.

The owner of the voice had cropped hair and tunnel eyes set far back in his head.

Everything about him seemed fake: his accent; his affected monastic hairstyle; his linen suit; even the plimsolls which provided a spring to his step.

He raised his hand, as if to slap Alexander on the arm in a brotherly manner, but failed actually to touch him, rather as women elsewhere in the room mimed extravagantly affectionate kisses at each other.

'How was New York?' inquired Alexander. He did not introduce Frank to Tessa. He wanted to keep Tessa to himself.

'Terrific. But they live too much in the future. Not even the present. Mind you, this place – England – stumbles about in the past with the lights off.'

Frank sat down, still staring straight ahead of him as if he was supplied with a pair of blinkers. He sent out one of his big pincer hands for the champagne bottle. A waitress appeared with a glass. 'And you know that little bitch sacked me. You see, I wouldn't let her tamper with my work.'

'Really, Frank?' said Alexander. 'I heard another story. I heard that she sacked you because every interview you did turned into an interview with yourself. The celebrities never got a look in.'

'So that's the rumour, is it?' He lit a cigarette. 'Something in it, of course,' he admitted. 'The people were all so dull. They spoke like automatons. Sometimes I didn't even go and see them. I knew the kind of things they'd say so I made it all up. I think that was a bit of a problem. Most just accepted the publicity but some caused trouble… anyway, it's all trivial… I'm writing a book about philosophy now… an analysis of how to live…' He settled down. 'It begins like this: "Little by little, as individualism increases, as the belief in a deity decreases, each man becomes more and more isolated, rigidifying into a series of gestures, seeing no reason to do good if he finds he prefers to do bad, discovering that his only way to be part of things is to be noticed. Thus one after the other falls prey to Satan's sin of hubris and humanity disintegrates into no more than a series of gestures, without unity, just a number of rigid figures like those found after the destruction of Pompeii."'

Frank was watching Tessa, to observe whether or not he had impressed her.

'Who are you?' he said to her. 'Ever since I walked through the door I have wanted to know who you are. We haven't met before, have we?'

She shook her head.

'Who are you though?'

'My name is Tessa Armstrong... Alexander here is intending to marry my mother. We have met here to discuss the matter – I wanted to dissuade him – but instead we have been constantly interrupted by assorted people. So I'm leaving.'

'Tessa Armstrong? Tom's daughter?' He grinned. 'You mean, Alexander, you're intending to marry the wife of the man you killed? I had no idea. Being abroad makes one a bit cut off. That must be very satisfying for you. I remember... you were always rather jealous of him, weren't you? Most people were, because he was such a good writer and such a decent person. He seemed to have the secret of happiness. He was always cheerful, always saw the best in everything and everyone. That sounds trite. But oddly enough he was never trite. Everyone liked him, and admired him simply because he was admirable. People do like decent people, you know; it's the great secret of our times. We all pretend to like those who are rotten, but we merely enjoy their company because they make us feel honourable by comparison. But Alex, you went a little further than that, didn't you? I remember you even once claimed an article of Tom's as your own.'

'You've been drinking,' said Alexander.

Frank was still grinning.

'Perhaps you think that if you marry Tom's wife you'll turn into him. You won't be you any more. You'll be Tom. I quite see your point. I wouldn't mind being Tom.'

'Tom's dead,' said Tessa.

'The amusing thing is,' said Frank, 'that Tom's reputation has increased since his death and poor Alexander's has declined. I keep seeing Tom's name mentioned as one of the great journalists of this decade. That must be so irritating for you, Alexander. But you know, people's reputations often increase after they die, especially if they die relatively young. Those who live on are considered ordinary because of their tenacity in clinging on to the dull old earth.'

'I'm leaving now,' said Tessa.

Alexander rose to his feet.

'Alone.'

Tessa touched Alexander lightly on the cheek. 'See you,' she said.

Before he could say anything, try to stop her, kiss her, she had withdrawn down the aisle beside the bar, and vanished, leaving him still standing up, fumbling with his money to pay the bill, while Frank watched him with the hard, desolate stare which was a characteristic of those who frequented the Club.

PART III

16

Tessa Armstrong

Tuesday 12 September

In bed with Martin that night, last night, after leaving Alexander, I could hear the sound of the cars across the park and the voices below. The noises came in and out of my consciousness as I slept and woke, slept and woke. They were oddly full of promise, of echoes of other lives. When you look out at the vast timeless trees and the green of Highbury Fields you can't believe that the shabby house can exist in such an environment.

Cockroaches hurry across the floor, through the dust. The flaked paint on the windowsill reveals bare, rotting wood. The lino is disintegrating at the edges. Dust fills every crevice of the house – in the furniture, at the edges of the stairs, on the mantels above the disused fireplaces.

I took a long time to fall asleep in Martin's arms. I thought of Alexander's desperate eyes. I didn't sleep long. I listened to the thump of my heart, the tick of the clock. I heard a train dying away in the distance and an aeroplane overhead. I lay in one position after another. My limbs stuck to Martin. My head searched for a cool patch of the pillow. Sometimes my body lay right to the edge of the bed, where it was less hot. But then that grew hot and I lay on my back, the air on my face, my eyes open. I curled up in a womb-like position, with my back to Martin. But still I couldn't sleep. He moaned. I turned to face him, watching his freckled nose twitch, his hair over the pillow. My arms touched the skin of his arm. Sticking together in the night.

Early in the morning he woke, and we made love.

The expression on his face was intense and savage and yet loving at the same time. It's as though everything is being experienced: all time, all loss, everything.

At seven the room was light. My feet were so cold I hardly dared get up. Shivering, naked on the lino, I got dressed. Outside the trees cast shadows in the early morning sunlight.

Martin was curled up in his bed with an old brown blanket hugged around him. In sleep he looked quite innocent, with his red ruffled hair and his hands clutching the blanket for protection. He was murmuring something and he sounded troubled too.

He didn't go to work today. He said he was giving it up.

'What will you do?'

'I think I shall pursue a political career,' he said.

Later today. Alexander rang. He said he was phoning to say he was not going to stop pursuing me – not ever.

'Who was that on the phone?' asked Martin.

'Oh – just that girlfriend of mine,' I said.

But perhaps my sly smile gave me away.

'I don't want you seeing her again,' snapped Martin. 'Never again.'

17

Martin Sherman

Tuesday 12 September

Sometimes it seems so comical. All these theories: of how we arrived here, which disasters caused the destruction of which species, that sixty-five million years ago the dinosaurs died out because the world was hit by an object from space and the dust covered everything. The magnitude of it all – while I and the rest of us spend our time like ants. Ants in suits and ties hurrying in and out of banks, in and out of offices. Men in swivel chairs spinning round, counting money, making figures grow on their computers, telephoning each other with information.

Yesterday I went into the City to see a money man. He had the roundest eyes I've ever seen. The rest of him doesn't seem to work properly – the limbs move slowly, the fingers are stiff, all the life is in those calculator eyes.

His office is bland. No books there. Grim smiles and money-spinning eyes. Not even a photograph of his wife or a mansion in Surrey: just a phone, a computer, a desk and a chair. Spiders in their webs.

He strokes the table. 'I can't invest money you haven't got.' (He's noted that I'm not one of them. I'm watching him closely to make sure I play my part better next time.)

I grin. 'Just remember,' I say. 'Remember the fund I mentioned today.'

'Look, Mr Sherman. I don't want to be rude but you must have money.'

'And you think I haven't got money? Why?'

'Just something about you. We learn to know these things.'

'Take my number. And – please – remember our conversation. I have no doubt that you'll be surprised in a day or two.'

The money-spinning eyes were closing in on me.

I stood up, grinning.

'I'm so sorry to waste your time,' I said. But I had been doing my research and, besides, I had a hunch. Since being with Tessa I have been listening hard, analysing more.

He stood up, or rather raised himself a little above his metal desk, and stuck out a dry hand. I shook it vigorously. Oh, I know I'm a bad person, I know I'm destructive, but at least I'm alive, whereas these men behind desks are growing small, inconsequential bodies below their Mekon heads. They have no strength left in them but I can swagger and grin. I can swindle and laugh. And I can charm. I can charm even this dull-skinned creature sunk behind his desk. Already I can see his mind buzzing with doubts. He knows there's more to me than swagger. He senses that I might be lucky and even he knows that there's more to this world of high finance than well-judged calculations.

He knows there wouldn't be so much laughter in my eyes if I wasn't certain he'd regret his mistake. In his life he has learnt to judge between real laughter and pretend laughter, and my laughter is always real, a deep-seated, constant sense of delight.

It is all so ridiculous, such a game, such a constant comedy, as people make their exits and entrances as though acting out one of those old farces. Enter – a baby. Exit – an old man. What a hoot. Why does everyone take it so seriously? This man, with his shrivelled hands, he's growing old here without any light.

I smile, and already he looks a little better, a little more real. Because I'm real, you see. That's where I'm different from the rest of them. Tessa and I, we're real, and powerful, and important, that's why people will be drawn to us. Of course, until I met Tessa I wasn't real, I was living a half-life, in the shadows, but now I've stepped out, swaggered out, into the sunlight.

TESSA ARMSTRONG

Wednesday 13 September

MARTIN WATCHES ME WITH HUNGER, AS THOUGH HE WANTS me to be all his, for always. I don't know if I could do without it, now. I like to be the object of men's desire. Without their desire I'm not real. I'm just a shape made of flesh, draped in clothes, with a brain ticking like a clock. With Martin's eyes on me I feel powerful again.

I walked this morning to Clissold Park where I noticed the delicate feet of the ducks, the white rabbits chasing each other in the wired pen, the sudden burst of light and rain which irradiated the sky. It all seemed breathtakingly temporary.

Slowly I went over to the fallow deer which tottered about on long legs and hooves like women on high heels. Their eyes were so docile, so trusting, that I felt guilty, terribly guilty, as if I were more than an onlooker, as if I were inextricably involved with the destruction of this planet.

The bare branches of the trees struggled in all directions against the indifferent sky.

Far away, a train rumbles along its metal tracks towards its many destinations and the house shakes a little.

Fragments in a world of division.

Martin says he will free me of my conscience.

Martin Sherman

Wednesday 13 September

I AM WRITING THIS WHILE TESSA SLEEPS. THE ROOM IS close, and a little clammy. Our washing is piled up in one corner. Tessa hasn't unpacked the suitcase which is on top of the wardrobe. It is night and I keep waking up hot and uncomfortable. I wish I knew everything about Tessa. I want her to be all mine; everything she has done, everything she will do. I want to know what she was like as a child, as an adolescent. I want to know the changing shades of her hair and her eyes. I want to know the kind of clothes she used to wear, the friends she used to have, the books she liked best.

I want to possess her completely.

Her suitcase is locked. I wonder why she keeps it locked.

I want to know who was her first lover, and who her last. I want to know what she did to them, and they to her.

20

Tessa Armstrong

Thursday 14 September

I KEEP STARING AT NOTHING AND THINKING OF MARTIN WITH a smile on my face. Either I'm thinking of things Martin has said or imagining things we'll do or contemplating my feelings. It's full-time. But what I like best is the dying light, the sunset being slowly blanketed by clouds, the darkness taking over.

As Martin pushes into me my body ripples out in ecstasy and I want more and more of it until my body is covered in sweat and I ache and there are juices streaming between my legs. I want him to make love to me everywhere. Between my breasts, in my armpits, in my mouth, everywhere. I want the dark pleasures everywhere. I want some pleasure, and then I want more. And after that still more. I cry out and want to cry out again and again until all I am is severed flesh and my voice crying out in pain and pleasure.

As we make love it almost seems that we are creating something else, or being created by something else, the lust is so strong, so much a presence oiling our bodies with its sweat. It is a little frightening, the power and the anger which brings our bodies to such high ecstasy in the blackness.

He always draws the curtains tightly and even cuts off the light from under the door with a cushion. He likes to make love in absolute darkness.

I lie on the bed, and I watch him go to the windows and draw the curtains and I watch him shut out the other light under the door. And I am aroused by his shape moving in the room, controlling me. And when the light is all gone I know we are again in our private world where anything can happen.

I had to stop myself crying out too loud as my face was last night plunged into the pillow and he thrust into me from behind. The savagery of our love-making links us darkly and forever. I need him. He helps me forget. Without him life would be reduced to its component parts.

And yet I still want to see Alexander again.

He phones me every day.

He swears that there was nothing between my mother and him until a year ago. But I wonder.

I keep thinking back, and wondering.

Could he really have had an affair with my mother before my father's death? His best friend's wife, along with his best friend's daughter?

I suppose I shall have to unlock that suitcase.

Before I left my mother's home last Saturday I went up to the attic to take a last look at my old dolls and the dressing-up box and my doll's house, and I saw the suitcase there, full of my father's papers. There was a small key in the rusty lock. Inside, the notebooks and letters were covered with dust and mice droppings and some letters had been gnawed at by the mice.

My mother should not have allowed my father's diaries and letters to get in this state. She didn't deserve him. She doesn't deserve these ghosts of his mind to remain with her.

For years I hadn't dared look at them, but I shall look now. I have nothing to lose. I used to think I had a soul to lose.

I carried the suitcase down, and added my own letters and diaries before locking it. A label stuck to it said 'Cunard – *The Queen Mary*' with a picture of a huge ocean liner.

Attics and cellars and suitcases, the corners of our minds, forgotten journeys, the beginning and the end of things.

The papers smelt of old time, worn-out time, lost hopes.

I wish he hadn't died. He was a good man.

Alexander destroyed my father's life, and now he is trying to destroy mine.

21

Martin Sherman

Friday 15 September

I HAD LUNCH WITH MY MOTHER TODAY, AT HER USUAL RES-taurant near the Houses of Parliament. It is dark and shadowy, like a gambler's den, and full of men in suits. They have a horrible range of necks: thin ones, thick ones, red ones.

An oil painting of a dog with a bleeding pheasant hanging from its mouth loomed down above me. All over the walls there were glistening Victorian oil paintings, mostly depicting human beings or their dogs chasing other creatures and killing them.

'Very atmospheric, isn't it?' I said.

'Shall we have a good red wine?' she asked.

Her face has been chipped out of granite: toneless skin, towering brow, firm jaw. Only the watchful, fluid little eyes are human. She wore a grey suit with a brown shirt, as though designed to be turned into a stone statue outside some civic centre.

She greeted an acquaintance by raising her hand as though it were extremely heavy and operated by a motor.

Her smile was like a sudden crack in a rock rather than being warm and likeable.

Waiters issued backwards and forwards bearing dishes steaming with the kind of food my mother used to cook for Sunday lunch before she gave up home for work: steak-and-kidney pie, lamb, plenty of vegetables.

There were no women except for my mother in the room, and the men, all in more or less identical suits, leant together over their tables in a conspiratorial manner. Many of them had very red faces, not from embarrassment but from alcohol consumption. Even the younger ones looked unhealthy, as though they spent all their time plotting in corners.

And yet the odd thing was that in spite of the conspiratorial air, I had never been in a restaurant where it had been easier to hear what was being said on other tables, which perhaps was the real reason people came here.

'The Whips will never wear it,' remonstrated one man.

'He thinks it'll be quite impossible unless we take Richard and the rest of them,' declaimed a voice from somewhere else.

'I'll have to ask my master about that,' whispered a third voice at a table further off.

The words hung around in the restaurant long after they had left the speakers, echoing slightly, before fading gradually away.

'It's amusing, all this, you know,' she said, 'influencing events.'

Her voice was much lower than the other voices. I could hardly hear it. Her eyes glittered like the oil paintings.

'I'm glad you're taking an interest in politics,' she continued. 'I always knew it would suit you.'

She signalled to a waiter, who took our order, bowing slightly as he did so.

The stout, slightly purple-skinned man on the table next to us was eating his way through a small brown bird.

I chose prawns then salmon, although my mother recommended the game.

She went on to describe one by one each of the men in the restaurant – what they did, what their views were, where they lived – and then their wives and mistresses.

'And just over there, talking to the appalling skinny Geoffrey Robuck, who by the way visits a prostitute every Wednesday night, there's Peter Ward, whose daughter Nicola was in trouble over some stupid lad she persuaded to jump off a bridge. The boy drowned. Poor Peter. He thinks no one knows. He has the most charming wife. A great asset.'

She straightened her napkin on her lap. 'Well, I must say, you do look very much smarter now. And there's something in your manner... a certain authority. I can't tell you what a relief it is to see you looking as I'd always envisaged you. For years, well, as you know, you have been a worry to us. Your clothes – always so scruffy. Your manner – so truculent and rude, as though you were laughing at your father and me and at the rest of the world.'

'Oh – I don't find things less funny. I am just learning to conceal my amusement.'

Her head was on one side as she scooped a spoonful of prawns into her mouth. She still had not learnt the art of applying make-up, and anyone feeding her would have been misled as to the position of her mouth because the lipstick was applied a little to the left of the opening. Her head was as coarse as it had always been, very roughly made, with eyes which were rather too small, thus heightening the appearance of having been knocked into shape overnight in a second-rate sculptor's studio.

'I'll never forget that awful visit we paid to your lodgings. We arrived unexpectedly – I believe we were having luncheon somewhere near.'

'Fulham. The other side of London. And I think your memory is at fault – you actually called round on a carefully planned raid to make sure I wasn't harbouring drugs or pornography or two girls or one man or any other such deviation from the norm. What I can never comprehend is why you – who are a living example of a deviation from the norm, a ruthlessly ambitious, intellectually brilliant woman who appears one hundred per cent conservative in everything she says and does yet is standing as a Labour candidate – why you should criticize me for abnormal behaviour.'

'I wasn't. I criticized you for not turning out as I'd expected. That is not at all the same as criticizing you for being abnormal.'

She was watching me closely. Her shoulders grew bigger and bigger day by day. The last time I saw my father, on the raid my mother mentioned, he was thinner and slighter, as though she were gaining strength taken from him. Perhaps she sucks his blood at night. He had shuffled into the room as though he were wearing his slippers.

I had enjoyed her visit. I enjoyed it rather too much. It occurred to me then that one reason I lived as I did was to irritate my mother. The other reason was the reason why Tessa had hidden herself away: I was scared of myself. I felt no guilt, as Tessa seems to feel guilt. But I was scared of my desire to burn things down. I was scared at the pleasure I took in destruction. It was easier not to exist, just to play at living, to manufacture some semblance of a life in that absurd house, in that ridiculous supermarket, and to make its point the prolonged irritation of my mother.

My poor mother. For a moment, as she watched me from the other side of the table, in the shadowy restaurant, she looked happy. Her son was back with her again, smiling at her, well dressed, wearing a tie, speaking whole sentences instead of the occasional retort. I told her a little about Tessa.

'Well, I'll meet her,' my mother said graciously. 'I'm having a party soon for a few local people and politicians – why don't you bring her along? She wouldn't be out of things, would she? Out of her depth I mean?'

'Oh no,' I said, 'I doubt very much if she would be out of her depth.'

She wiped a bit of dead bird from her lips with her white napkin.

'Well, you must definitely come… besides, you might like to meet a few of my friends now you've turned so eminently respectable.'

'Certainly,' I said.

She looked at me severely. 'You know... you should bear in mind that money could help my political career considerably. You should bear that in mind.'

'What do you mean?'

'If you were ever to get rich, if anything were to happen to make you very rich.'

'What exactly have you in mind?'

'Your uncle... he's not well. He might be dying. It's one of the things I wanted to talk to you about. He told me he's considering leaving you everything.'

'How very kind,' I said. I tried not to smile.

'He told me he wanted to leave it to you because you would cause most trouble with it. He... appears very angry with the world.'

'I don't blame him. It's an annoying place.'

'Do you care that your uncle's dying?'

'Oh yes. What exactly is the matter with him?'

'He won't say. He just says he's dying... cancer, I suppose.'

'I see.'

'You will be careful, won't you, Martin?' she said, leaning forward like a vulture. 'In establishment life it is important never to reveal a lack of conscience or a deficiency of compassion. It is vital to appear to live up to the highest standards while equally vital to live up to no such thing.'

We ate more and spoke more until she looked at her watch in alarm.

I said goodbye to her outside the Houses of Parliament just as it began to drizzle. She kissed me on the cheek, and I could have sworn that she blushed.

The Houses of Parliament looked majestic, rising up there full of lighted windows like an advent calendar, busy with desks and people, all rushing about planning and plotting, making their careers or reforms, answering letters, trying to keep England running smoothly. Envelopes and paperwork.

A policeman was walking towards me, about to move me on.

In Gene Kelly mood I danced and walked all the way home causing stares and consternation among the tourists and looks in the other direction from the residents.

What a dull old place England is, I thought. It needs waking up. The whole world needs waking up.

When I got home Tessa seemed pleased at the news about my uncle, but not as pleased as I'd hoped.

'You look so thrilled, Martin. How it is you care for me and yet nobody else?'

She turned away.

'I can be better,' I said.

If I married her, then I'd be certain of her. Then I might have her forever. You see, I want to possess her soul as well as her body. But sometimes she seems far away, thinking about someone else. Perhaps it's Alexander, perhaps it's her father.

22

TESSA ARMSTRONG

Friday 15 September

WHILE MARTIN WAS AT LUNCH WITH HIS MOTHER, I TOOK out the suitcase.

I sorted through my father's letters. There were yellowing bills, receipts, letters from his father, one or two from his mother. Valentine cards, a pressed rose, newspaper cuttings.

Some of the newspaper cuttings had Alexander's name on them too because they wrote together. I bet Alexander refers to them as his articles now.

There was one notebook which seemed to contain interviews about the IRA, a mixture of shorthand and longhand. Another notebook was all in shorthand.

It was the third notebook which interested me most. Even before I opened it I knew... there was something about it... the careful way the date was written on a label stuck to the front cover... even the smell of it: it smelt of paper and ink and privacy, whereas the other notebook stank of other people, cigarettes and talk.

It was written in brown ink, with firm round handwriting.

A diary, started just two weeks before he died.

I made myself a cup of coffee before sitting on the bed (unmade) to read it.

It began in rather a cramped, formal manner:

I am accustomed to write about public affairs and have never been an expert on private ones. I tend to live my life as it comes and not spend a great deal of time in prying into my motives and those of others. However, in recent months I have been feeling the need to write certain things down, so here it is, a diary – something I have always avoided. But perhaps if I can write about my life as I write about other people's lives, report it from a distance, as a journalist, I can come to some kind of understanding.

Last night it became clear to me that I must start writing things down when I found myself confiding in a taxi driver. Let me bore the paper instead of boring strangers.

I started to talk expansively to him on the way to a dinner. It has never been my habit to talk like this, and I observed my own behaviour with interest. Usually it is taxi drivers who talk on and on at me.

As I talked I leant forward slightly, as though it was important I get my message across to the big-necked man in the seat in front.

'Do you know, at the moment I keep getting all kinds of extraordinary ideas and insights. Do you ever get periods like that?'

'No sir, I can't say I do,' replied the man's heavy voice warily.

'It's as though most of the time we go around double-glazed and sound-proofed and then, suddenly, for a combination of reasons, it all goes, all the sound-proofing, and we can more or less hear the grass grow.'

'Really sir?'

'One can think more clearly. One can have exhilarating perceptions because one's brain is no longer trapped in that sound-proofed cell. Do you see my point?'

The man grunted.

'You see, recently, for various reasons, which I won't go into, I've been thinking quite a bit about God and the devil, good and evil, morality, if you like. And my brain seems to be getting clearer.

'But sometimes all kinds of odd things come into my brain, things I simply haven't thought of before. This is one example – are you listening? – supposing God did trigger off the explosion which created our universe? A theory which is perfectly plausible and consistent with known scientific facts. But supposing the devil is God's child and the naughty child was furious to discover the only bauble he had to play with was earth, that none of the other planets had any life on them at all.

'The devil had to make his games last, of course, because earth was all he had until the universe contracted back into God's black handkerchief and God once more said a few spells and flung the handkerchief open to reveal another universe of stars and planets and new galaxies for his child to play with.

'But the devil had to wait a long time for that new set of playthings, many millions of years, so he had to keep things going on earth, give them the means for destruction but try to prevent them using it, to amuse himself.

'Of course there is always the possibility, just the possibility, that the devil might grow up enough to let us be. On the other hand he might smash us all in a petulant sulk if we bored him.

'It's the bright, bad people who keep the devil amused, you see, and that's why everyone admires bad people: they keep the devil amused and prevent his destroying us all.

'But we could all be destroyed so easily – by an irresponsible politician, a few stupid technicians, by an unnecessary war. And, of course, by a meteorite or another ice age or a plague.'

There was a long silence from the taxi driver, who had been negotiating a dense bit of traffic.

'Are you a member of a particular religious sect?' he inquired eventually.

I sank back in my seat. 'Oh no. Not at all. Not at all.' I looked out of the window. How beautiful it all looked: the blanketing darkness of the evening, the people hurrying home, the intensity with which people lived their lives. London was a breathing, living, city that night, gusting its inhabitants along its streets, up its stairs, into its shops selling alcohol.

Even there in the City in a wreck of old and new buildings, there was plenty of life, shifting, varied life, old men in mufflers and young boys in leather jackets, old women in overcoats and girls with stylish hair.

Someone was walking their dog, someone else was drunk. Respectability and grubbiness joined together here, as everywhere in London.

And all around, from every dark corner, from down every narrow alleyway, the past waited.

'It's odd how one sees things at the wrong times, isn't it? That some people spend their lives realizing things at the wrong times, when it's too late or too early, when the experience is all over or hasn't happened. Perhaps it's living in London, with its strong sense of the past, which makes so many of us live our lives in retrospect instead of in the present.'

The man made no comment.

Who is this man? I thought. Who are all these men who ferry one about between the various worlds we live in? Often we don't even see their faces. Blank faces, blank voices, ferrymen.

'It is very foolish, I think,' I said out loud, a little afraid of the silence, 'to realize things too late. Do you have children?'

'No. No children.'

'Well, I have two. Stephen, who is twenty, and Tessa who is fifteen. They're lovely children. Only I don't see them much. I'm away a lot you see.'

I remembered when Tessa was born, I had wanted to show her everything. I had read up about the origins of life, about dinosaurs and fossils and even tried to learn the names of butterflies, to teach Tessa when she was older.

Wide-eyed, marvelling, Tessa had staggered about astonished by everything she saw, in particular by the way dogs urinated. I had kept pointing up at the stars, which were too far off for Tessa's attention quite yet; the close-up world of ants and dogs and spiders was enough for a while.

But newspapers dragged me back. Black-and-white words recording events without emotion – analysis and understanding and facts, facts, facts. Tessa had had no interest in facts. She just liked to watch how things happened for her, and make things happen for her. She wanted to discover her own world, not her father's second-hand one. 'Tessa do it' she would cry when someone was about to switch on the television. 'Tessa do it' when someone drew a face for her. Once I pointed out to her where England was on the map and Tessa had frowned and hurled the map away.

'She's too young for all that. She doesn't know where her house is yet,' Marian had said.

And as for me, I had thought then, do I know so much more?

As the taxi proceeded past Sadler's Wells, down Theobald's Road, past closed shops and dark offices, it seemed that I was driving away from them, and that in doing so I was pulling away from life itself.

My children had seen everything as important, but I found it impossible to crouch down with them and look up and see the grandeur of the kitchen table, the wonder of the cat slinking along the wall, the astonishment as a lorry went by.

Yet that was surely where heaven lay: seeing a world in a grain of sand and a heaven in a wild flower. Hell is losing that perspective.

I thought again of Tessa when she was little, the way she swung her arms as she walked as though she controlled the world, as though she had inherited it all, as though it were all hers – which in a way it was.

When Tessa was born she had had all time in her eyes like some ancient guru who had been here since the world began and yet had only just arrived.

Sometimes Tessa would stare into space as though remembering some other time, some other place, her face flooded with that curious inner light which never left her, even when she was plotting something wicked.

I saw Tessa, as a two-year-old, jumping up and trying to put a leaf back which had fallen from a tree.

I saw the expression on her face when she first stepped onto a beach and crouched down to run her fingers through the sand.

Even when she was tiny, she would descend to greet our guests for dinner as though she were royalty. At five she would graciously engage them in conversation while poor Stephen lurked shy, resentful, upstairs. Once a friend called round while we were in the garden. She invited him in and asked what he wanted to drink. He jokingly requested a dry martini. She went to the drinks cabinet and prepared one (she had seen me make them, I suppose) which her guest claimed was the best he had ever tasted. She then walked, in that stately way of hers, into the garden to summon us in. She was just six years old.

I can still see that formal little figure, her hair tied back in a long pony tail, coming down the lawn towards us. 'Father, your friend Peter Warwick has called round about the lawn mower. I prepared him a small dry martini before coming out, as he looked thirsty.' I remember Marian's eyes flashing at me with the alarm I had seen so many times before – when Tessa started walking at six months, when she spoke full sentences at one, when she started reading just before her third birthday, always with that sense of precision. She didn't even babble like other babies before she spoke: her words came out fully formed, articulate, and full of an earnest charm.

'It's not natural,' said Marian to me as we walked back to the house. 'It just is not natural.'

'Excuse me,' Tessa said when she had gathered us together in the drawing room, with the window seat looking over the garden, where the weeping willow weeps into a small dank pond. 'I think I should get back to my dolls. One of them is being systematically tortured by the others.'

She smiled apologetically before leaving, with what I could have sworn was a slight, courtly, bow.

She wasn't much older the day I discovered that her dolls had acquired a silver tea set.

I stood over her up in the playroom as she poured each of the dolls a cup of tea and put in imaginary sugar from the silver sugar bowl.

'Where did you get that tea set?'

She didn't answer.

'I said where did you get it?'

'You'll make them spill their tea if you upset them by using that tone of voice.'

I crouched down. 'Darling – I said where did you get that lovely tea set?'

She looked at me with those drowning green eyes of hers. 'The window was open so I went in. Let's keep them, shall we, Daddy? Let's not tell Mummy.'

'What window?'

'The window of one of the houses that back on to ours. An old lady lives there. I think she might be a witch. I doubt if she deserves such lovely silver, anyway. Her house smelt of cats.'

'Tessa – you can't just walk into people's houses and take whatever you want.'

'Why not? Why can't I, Daddy? It was very easy. Many things you say I can't do I find very easy to do. Esmerelda… do you want any more tea? It's from the very best stolen silver.'

She grinned at me. 'Only the best for Esmerelda,' she said.

In spite of a tantrum from Tessa, we returned the silver.

Odd that I loved her so much, that I love her so much. It's her spirit I love – the unconquerable human will.

'The unconquerable human spirit…'

'Anything the matter, mate?' said the cab driver.

I realized I had my head in my hands.

'It's my daughter.'

'I'm sure she can look after herself.'

'That's what my wife says. She says my daughter's been flirting with my best friend. She's only fifteen.'

'Good-looking is she, your daughter?'

'Very.'

'That can annoy mothers. We're here. At Langan's.'

I stopped reading. I found it too distressing.

23

MARTIN SHERMAN

Sunday 17 September

TESSA HAS BEEN DISTANT, AND SECRETIVE. I SUGGESTED WE spend a night in Brighton, for a change. I wanted to get away from the brooding atmosphere of Hope Villa.

Mrs Monson is cultivating a martyred air. She hasn't washed her grey brillo-pad hair for weeks and her apron is filthy. She keeps muttering about reporting me to the social services. She doesn't seem to understand that she no longer owns the house.

'It's that girl,' she said to me yesterday. 'She's done all this, hasn't she?'

'All what?'

'This was my parents' house. I kept a decent house. And now you two come here – shaking the house and playing your music.'

'We don't play music. That's the twins.'

She wiped her hands covered in flour over her face (she is responding to the crisis by making cakes and biscuits, always rock hard).

'I don't like this sort of behaviour in my house,' she said. 'All that... sex.'

She looked shocked, as though amazed to hear herself say the word.

'Have you been listening again, Mrs Monson, standing on the stairs listening?'

'Of course not – but I've heard. It's impossible not to hear. And this is my house. All these disgraceful goings on – and the atmosphere, Martin, the atmosphere, it's changed. It's all wrong now. She's made my house go wrong – she and that horrible smile of hers. I know it isn't you. It couldn't be you. You've always been a good boy – so sympathetic. It couldn't be you.'

'Could I put you straight on one particular, Mrs Monson?' I said. 'It's actually not your house. It's mine. You sold it to me. The money's in your bank now.'

'I don't want the money. I want my house,' she said. 'I won't move.'

'You have flour all over your face, Mrs Monson,' I said.

She swung round, and waddled off down the hall to her rooms, which smell of cooking. Homely smells to cover up the smell of death and betrayal.

As for Mr Phillips, he has locked himself in and won't speak to me, although why he wants to stay in that fossilized room with the sloping roof I don't know.

A Bible squats beside his bed like a black spider.

To drown the knowledge of what they have agreed to, the twins play their music extra loudly (I have paid them a small sum to leave their attic room).

'You can't hide your lying eyes… Heading for the cheating side of town.'

I am not worried that they are all refusing to leave. I do have a plan.

The house is insured for a great deal of money – far more than I paid for it.

Brighton had an abandoned air. On the pier almost everything was closed. Stalls – with signs joyfully announcing candy floss, strawberries, personally engraved key rings, waffles – were boarded up. The dodgems, the ghost train, the hall of mirrors, just stood on the deserted pier waiting for summer. A cold wind from the sea bit into us as we walked beside the lacy railings holding hands.

I wouldn't let Tessa bring her father's diaries with us.

There was a man in a wheelchair in front of us and we both avoided looking at him. He was muffled up in a woolly hat and rug.

The amusement arcade was open and we spent some minutes putting pennies into slots and losing them. A few dissolute young men in leather jackets were hanging around the white hall; one or two old ladies and gentlemen were gambling away their pensions on the fruit machines.

Outside, through the window, I could see the apricot light of the sunset sandwiched between heavy clouds and the sea. It was being squeezed out. Soon there would be only the dark blend of sky and sea.

'You shouldn't be so upset about your mother marrying,' I told Tessa.

'He killed my father. Traditionally, people do tend to get a little peeved when the man who kills their father marries their mother.'

She slammed another coin into a fruit machine and pulled the handle.

'It was a long time ago.'

'It wouldn't matter if it were a dozen lifetimes away. He killed my father. And my mother broke his heart.'

'Whose heart?'

Five oranges appeared on the fruit machine and coins clattered furiously out.

'Oh look – I've won the jackpot… My father's heart.'

'How do you know?'

'I guess. I guess from his papers. I don't know.' She scooped up the coins.

'You shouldn't read those papers. They only depress you. You should concentrate on our life now. Your past one is finished.'

'Not quite. He loved me a lot, you know.'

'Leave the machine alone… come on.' I put my hands around her waist and nestled my lips into her neck. I pushed my hands up, to cover her breasts, and she moaned a little.

I could sense the arcade attendant glaring from his little box. But not enough happened in Brighton in the autumn to make him lose the opportunity of this free entertainment, so he didn't stop us.

She turned, and dragged my lips down on to her lips.

We were staying in a boarding house. For some reason she insisted on staying there instead of a smart hotel.

'I like seedy places,' she had said. 'I'm used to them. We belong here, hiding in corners, staring out at the sea from badly furnished rooms.'

We walked back there, walking so close it was hard to walk, and we hurried up to the room where the bed was unmade and smelling of the sex we had had when we first arrived.

That afternoon, watching the dolphins spin and jump, I felt quite carefree. But in the main hall of the aquarium we saw a thuggish Groupie fish covered in black spots who glowered out of his tank as if there were someone imprisoned in his body for multiple murders.

In another tank, a piranha floated wicked and bloated in the solitude of his cell.

We walked along by the sea and watched the surf and listened to the scramble of the pebbles as the waves pulled away. Clouds were closing in. Quite a long way ahead, up on the promenade, I could see the man in the wheelchair being pushed along.

She walked back to the boarding house staring at the ground.

Our room had a television and a big double bed. Silently, fully clothed, we lay on the bed with all the lights on and my fingers traced the secrets of her body over her face.

We kissed and I wanted that kiss to go on and on. I wanted that kiss to last forever. It seemed unbearable that it should end, that each act of love had to end, that we could only be fused for a few moments, that one day we would be separated by death.

At dinner that evening neither of us ate much. We sat on the first floor of a Chinese restaurant and the lanterns hanging from the ceiling swayed gently as if from the currents of conversation filling the shabby room.

In the street outside, a motorbike started up.

The sea was only a short walk away. By now it would be invisible except for the breaking surf white in the night.

'I think,' I said, 'that we should plan our lives together. As a team.'

'Is that a marriage proposal?'

'It's much more than that.'

'Perhaps,' she said.

24

Tessa Armstrong

Sunday 17 September

'We two, we spend our time high up, looking down on others. Other people don't matter to us,' I said. 'We see them from a distance, as insects we can just step on.'

Martin put his arms around my waist and whispered, 'Always standing by windows, always staring out. Turn towards me.'

He took my shoulder and pulled me round to face him. 'That's what you're like, Tessa,' he said; 'you can't help it.'

'I should try to. We both should. My father…'

'Your *father*. You go on about him as though he were the Lord Almighty – that diary of his is the Bible, is it?'

'Stop it. You're hurting my shoulder.'

'Well stop being so foolish. You and I, we've found each other,' he said.

'But you and I, we don't care about anything. We're dangerous.'

'Dangerous! What do we do that's so dangerous?'

'Darling, whatever you have done, whatever you will do, I can see it in your eyes.'

He let go of me and I turned back to the window. The wind was making the leaves on the trees shiver and sending a few leaves hurrying through the air.

He put his arms around my waist again, and kissed my ear.

'You could never leave me even if you wanted to. We need each other, you and I.'

'You're planning something, aren't you, Martin?'

I could hear his breathing, very even, behind me.

'And you – my sweet – are so virtuous?'

'I have no plans.'

'You should stop reading your father's diaries. They make you miserable.'

'He was a good man. He loved me.'

The day suddenly darkened as a shower of rain filled the air outside the rattling window.

'Look at the people running for cover,' said Martin contemptuously. 'They're all so afraid of getting wet.'

'So – is that so ridiculous?'

'Everything is ridiculous.'

I pulled away from him.

'Except you,' he said, grinning. 'You're older, and colder, and far more intriguing than any of them.' He crossed his arms. 'Look at you now: your grey hair, that haughty face and your eyes – black and icy.' He moved a step closer to me, and touched my skirt. 'Even your clothes – grey silk. Sometimes you seem made of grey silk – of fogs and clouds. And sometimes it seems that if I touched you all I'd feel is a kind of cold dampness, the sense of something that's already gone or not just come. But when I do touch you, you know, my stomach lurches, my heart pounds, every centimetre of my skin begins to shiver. It's desire, of course. But it doesn't feel like desire. It feels more urgent, as though you might evaporate if I didn't make all your flesh mine, and your soul.'

He was holding me close, burying his face in my hair.

'I shall never be all yours, Martin.'

25

MARTIN SHERMAN

Monday 18 September

'MY DARLING,' I SAID TO TESSA, 'YOU SEEM TO INSPIRE rather dreadful passions. If you were to join me at this window you'd see poor old Alexander Bartley standing by the ice cream hut and gazing up at our window with the air of a small boy who indeed wants an ice cream.'

'Ah yes,' she said, without coming to the window. 'I often see him there.'

'Doesn't his presence annoy you?'

'No. Not really.'

'I think you're lying.'

'I am trying not to be angry.'

'Well, my sweet, you can stay here, if you like, being the adorable daughter I've no doubt your father never had. But I'm going to go and have a talk with your suitor out there.'

'Leave him alone. Perhaps if we leave him alone it'll all pass over.'

'Pass over? He's come back to haunt your life. Look at him out there – it's pathetic. He's your father's killer and he's taken over your father's house, your father's wife. Now look closely – is he wearing your father's clothes? That'll be the next step – he'll start wearing his shoes, his socks, his jackets, his smile. He wants to be him, you know. I'm surprised you can put up with it. I'm going to have a talk with him. I don't like him worrying you. I won't be long.'

Before approaching Alexander Bartley, I watched him from close by. He didn't notice me. He was a man in a dream. He wore a big navy coat, and his tarnished gold curls hung forlornly over his face, blotchy from the cold.

He looked like any one of the desolate people who hang around public parks watching and waiting to break the loneliness and monotony and occasional insanity of their existences.

He didn't see me come towards him.

'Hello,' I said.

He jumped.

'Remember me?'

'Ah yes… I was just…' He looked at his watch.

I took his arm. 'I very much wanted a chat. I do hope it'd be no trouble.'

'Look I…'

'Must be going? Surely not quite yet. From the way you were standing there, it looked as though you had all the time in the world…'

'Well, I…'

'I expect you know lots of people who lived round here, in these fine terraces: journalists, publishers, lawyers, your sort of people. They all strike me as very content, very… self-satisfied. But maybe that's an illusion. You see, I'm the sort who looks through the windows and watches them as I go by. I see their Sanderson wallpaper, their subtle lighting, their spacious dining tables. They seem to have tamed life. Do you understand what I mean? I loathe that. They sit around eating their lightly cooked mangetouts discussing politics, the latest books, the new restaurants. And I hate them… You used to be like that, didn't you, before you met Tessa?'

'A bit.'

'And now – look at you – your hair blowing about like King Lear on the heath. It makes me laugh. It is so easy to lose control, isn't it? They think they've tamed it all but they haven't. Any one of those men, if subjected to Tessa for even a short period, could be like you, stumbling about on a cute little park turned wild heath...'

'Look, I'm just taking a quiet walk... I'm fine. I'm perfectly happy...'

'You know, I hope you don't mind my saying this but I've been surprised,' I said, 'that you have so much time to waste hanging round my house. But I suppose... since the tragic death of Tessa's father... you're not in any great demand at work. It must put people off a bit. But goodness he's doing well, isn't he? Even better in death than in life.'

Alexander blinked at me and seemed to come out of his daze. 'Look here...'

'Tell me, are you still in love with Tessa? Is that what the matter is?'

He pushed some strands of hair off his face in a nervous gesture. His fingers were stained yellow from smoking.

'No. Of course not. She's going... to be my daughter, that's all. I have a responsibility towards her. I just came here, to see if she was all right. As for Tom... of course, I'm delighted...'

'I thought you said you were just having a little walk.'

'Well yes, but while I was walking I thought I might... just look up at the window... of the house where she lived in case...'

'You caught a glimpse of her?... Well, I'll tell you something. She's my girlfriend. And I'd rather you left her alone and returned to your mangetouts and the Sanderson wallpaper. That's much safer.'

He looked straight at me, shook his head, and smiled slightly. 'I can't now.'

'No, I suppose you can't,' I admitted.

'Look, I just want to make sure that you're treating her well. She's very... sensitive.'

'Strange how men always call the most savage women sensitive, just so long as they're beautiful. That's what we all want, isn't it? Beauty. Not truth or goodness. Just beauty, ideally savage, spectacular beauty. Because we all sooner or later get bored with the dinner parties and the civilized chat. We want fires and storms and disasters and a woman like Tessa. But she's not for you. She and I, we understand each other. You should leave her alone.'

'You think I might take her away from you, don't you?' he said.

He laughed, and kicked over a pile of leaves. He at once looked younger, mischievous, irreverent.

'You're nervous,' he continued. 'You're not completely certain of her. That's why you came out to see me. Good heavens, I thought you were secure in her affections. You're afraid she might love me.'

He was smiling, and I could now see something of his attraction, a certain seedy charm. Even his hands, although they were stained yellow from cigarettes, were lover's hands, big and soft. He stood a little taller.

'Leave her alone,' I said. 'Just leave her alone.'

I turned and walked away from him. My fists were clenched tightly.

'Give her my love,' I heard him cry from behind me.

I looked up, to see her face at the window.

26

TESSA ARMSTRONG

Tuesday 19 September

As soon as Martin went out today I started reading again. Once more I found it too upsetting to read for long. The next few entries were full of politics – which minister had said what to whom, what topics had been discussed at a top-level lunch.

And then all of a sudden he broke off and wrote:

Every now and again I get a great sense of distance, as though I'm seeing things from a long way off. It's very… peculiar. I keep seeing flashes of earth a long way off. Such a pretty planet it looks. The only colour in the black void of space. Very round, and fragile and beautiful. That is what one forgets sometimes: that everything really is very important; that we are very lucky to be here. I am glad my son is an astronomer working on the real scale of things, the grand scale. I can't understand what Marian means when she says astronomy reduces things, turns us all into ants. That's seeing things from the wrong direction. We should be looking out to the skies, not in at ourselves, like the people here, shuffling from table to table, drink to drink, with tiny, half-closed eyes. We are part of the universe, that is the point. We belong here.

The likelihood of life appearing on earth was infinitesimal and the likelihood of me turning up even more improbable.

We have already won a universal lottery against staggering odds. That is what we forget.

Right now I feel many miles away. It's as though I'm suffering from some undisclosed illness which is making me see everything differently, from another perspective. And yet the distance doesn't belittle earth. Quite the opposite.

Supposing, just supposing, we really were the only life in the universe. Time and space went on and on through galaxy after galaxy, and perhaps there was only earth, spinning there, odd little inconsequential, precious earth.

And perhaps, if the earth were harmed, all that there was would be harmed. There is only life, after all, and if life is only on earth, we really are the centre of the universe. A tiny pinball in space – nothing at all, and yet maybe everything there is.

That quick, slow, everlasting twist of DNA. Spirals of life leading everywhere, staircases to heaven and hell.

Perhaps we are all there is. If that is so, every action each individual makes is a huge event, something of universal consequence.

I had a talk with Alexander last night.

'What science and astronomy shows is that we might well be all there is, and all there has been, ever,' I said to him; he looked bored. 'If only you realized just how important you are, we all are, everything would be so much better. You wouldn't behave shoddily – not that you do.' (In fact I do think Alexander behaves shoddily, to women in particular – although I suppose I quite admire his sense of freedom.)

'I could never be good like you,' Alexander said, lounging back smugly in his chair and lighting another cigarette.

'That's not the *point*. What I'm trying to make you understand is your *importance*. We're not little grubs in a vast black night. As far as we know we're the lords of the universe, all there ever has been and will be. I don't mean just human beings. But life on earth. That's wonderful, isn't it? Even you must think that's wonderful. And once you realize all this, everything changes. It's why I wanted my son to be an astronomer. The more we know, the more magnificent it is to exist, even to have existed, to be part of all this.' I gestured grandly, forgetting I was in the cramped bar of a Belfast hotel as I spoke. But as I gestured I believe that for a moment, just for a moment, Alexander was caught up in the illusion and saw a certain splendour in the dark corners and the pints of beer squatting heavily on the tables. 'The chances of life arriving were very small,' I continued. 'Surely you realize how fortunate you are, how fortunate each person born is, merely to exist within eternity, for however short a time.'

'I can't say I'm not pleased to be here,' said Alexander, wiping the beer from his mouth. 'I have a great time. I'm very lucky. For one thing,' he continued, 'that couple of girls who have just walked into the bar are wearing too much make-up to be altogether respectable. That's what I call luck.'

I frowned, and then I laughed. 'It's people like you who keep the devil amused – otherwise he might have smashed us all in a petulant sulk years ago.'

'Perhaps that's why the dinosaurs were wiped out,' said Alexander. 'They sound very boring creatures… if it had been up to me I'd have certainly eliminated them with an ice age or a meteorite.'

'You know,' I said, 'Hell is losing hope… it's seeing everything as inconsequential.'

'So what? Do stop talking like this, it's not like you. Why are you talking like this?' said Alexander, lighting a cigarette. 'What are you on about? You've seemed so disturbed recently. What is it?'

'Something Marian said to me,' I said, looking down. 'About our marriage.'

When I looked up I saw Alexander's face was white.

He bought me another drink and then went off to talk with the girls. Today at work he avoided me.

27

Martin Sherman

Sunday 24 September

Tessa accompanied me to one of my mother's drinks parties today in Epsom... None of the men could keep their eyes off her. What an excellent pair she and I make. Really, with her beauty and my luck there's nothing we two couldn't do. But she's fighting me off. Or perhaps it is her father who is fighting me. But one way or another, there's a battle going on, and it's for Tessa's soul. I don't know if she understands this or not. I've seen her looking at me oddly sometimes, as if she is beginning to guess. If only she'd see how much pleasure she and I would have if only she gave up fighting against the part of her that sins.

All the men, they wanted her. Every one of them. Even my father, my kindly, complacent father. I saw him watching her with longing.

A smile from her and any of those men would do as she wanted, whatever she wanted, whatever we wanted if we were a partnership. I need her, and she needs me too. I know she needs me. She doesn't know it perhaps, but she's been looking for me all her life because I can free her from all guilt. Together, we need never worry about what we have done because we would forgive each other anything.

In the station car park, the cars were frosted over. We took a taxi across Epsom Downs to my parents' house. A few determined walkers were striding over the bleak expanse of grass with their collars up and their dogs bounding towards each other. There were kites high in the windy sky. As a child I'd walked here with my parents and brother most Sundays and we'd attended nearly every race meeting, including the Derby. Even in those days, I'd been lucky. I'd always felt someone was on my side. I used to dream of political power. I wanted to be prime minister, I recall, and was convinced that I could be, if I chose. The idea of money and influence appealed to me. You see, I'd always liked to control other people, which is one reason I suppose why I enjoy fire and destruction.

I don't need to control Tessa. She and I, we would be a partnership if only she would let me.

The party was far grander than I'd imagined. The last time I'd been to one of my parents' parties was five years ago and sherry had been served. A few neighbours had stood around making dull conversation and eating peanuts. This time it was good white wine and fanciful canapés.

When we arrived the drawing room was already crowded. The vast picture window looked out on to the garden. The immaculate lawn and well-pruned trees were still and silent in the wintry light.

The light had a curious effect on everyone's features. It made the women's make-up look too obvious and it discoloured the men's faces. My father's drab face lit up when he saw us enter. He was standing by the window talking to a pretty old lady. Everyone looked much less dull and well meaning than my parents' past guests. Even the pretty old lady had a sharp blue stare. I noticed that the room had been redecorated. The floral wallpaper had gone and had been replaced by a Regency stripe with matching curtains.

'Oh God,' boomed out a loud voice. 'I couldn't agree with you more...'

A brash laugh issued from the other side of the room and then was lost in the general high-pitched drone. It was odd, the absolute calm of the late September day through the window, and on this side the hectic babble of voices.

'Hello, Martin,' said my father.

'This is Tessa. Tessa, this is my father.'

'How do you do? How very nice to meet you,' he said shaking her hand fervently. He was staring at her. He leant back on his heels, his face a road map of wrinkles.

'I'm delighted to meet you,' said Tessa. Her face was pearl white and severe.

My father looked shy and craned his neck. 'Martin, your mother's here somewhere. Quite a party this, heh? Can't say I know too many people. Mostly your mother's friends. Ah, I see her, she's with the local MP. Powerful chap. John Bullard's his name. Ah... she's coming over. We're expecting a few journalists too, but they're always late, those chaps.'

My mother was surging towards us like a battleship through the sea. She was radiant. She had always enjoyed controlling people and parties suited her talents very well.

'Do congratulate her on the party,' whispered my father. 'She's very pleased with the turnout. Lord this, MPs, Sir somebody somebody. Influential people. Right wing as well as left. Important not to be too militantly left, she thinks. Quite astonishing how many have turned up.'

In a gust of forced emotion, my mother kissed my cheek. My father was taken aback by the display.

'And this must be Tessa,' she said patronizingly. 'How delightful. I never get a chance to meet Martin's girlfriends.'

'How do you do, Mrs Sherman?' said Tessa with a quick smile. Already a number of men were watching Tessa. She wore a black dress and her hair was loose, falling like smoke down her shoulders.

'Darling,' said Mrs Sherman to her husband. 'Do fill their glasses.' He came back with a bottle in each hand. It was as though he had finally assumed the position she had been pushing him towards all these years: that of her butler.

'Have you known each other long then?' said my mother.

'Not long,' said Tessa.

My father was wandering about filling glasses and stopping to mop his brow every now and again.

I watched my mother greet ingratiatingly a man whose face was often seen on television.

My brother Henry's little fair-haired son was sitting with his arms crossed on the sofa watching with distaste. Everyone seemed to be gesticulating and shaking hands and throwing back their heads with braying laughter.

'Has your mother always been interested in politics?' said Tessa.

'No. But she's always been interested in power.'

'I'm amazed she's left wing. She doesn't seem it.'

'She's whatever's wanted. She'll help me if that's what we want. Come on. Let's talk to some of them. They're probably not so bad.'

'Oh – I expect they're pretty bad,' she replied.

We joined my brother and his wife who were with a young man who was talking very fast and enthusiastically as though trying to see how many words he could fit into a minute. He hardly paused to say hello and Henry's wife Annabel just nodded at Tessa and then kept surreptitiously glancing at her while we were listening to the young man's never-ending flow of words. He was an executive in an oil company. He was clearly very successful.

'Let's go outside,' Tessa said, 'I don't care much for talk about cars.'

As we made our way out we passed my mother who asked me for a private word. While we spoke three men gathered round Tessa, all standing closer than they should have, all looking more lustful than was fitting on a Sunday morning. Tessa stood there, very demure.

I suddenly heard her voice ring out: 'You are all so badly dressed. Why is that?'

I glanced round at the three men who looked down at their clothes then up into Tessa's laughing eyes.

She smiled at them, as though in pity.

The bald one looked as though he'd just seen a vision of the Madonna. His flaccid skin lost a few tones of colour.

The smaller man, in his early thirties, suddenly abandoned his air of dreary boredom. He gave Tessa a radiant, boyish, grin.

The third one, a stout fellow who had approached Tessa simply because the others had looked puzzled and disorientated. He sank slightly in his flesh.

'You're Tessa Armstrong, aren't you?' said the small man. 'I knew your father. I saw you at one of his parties. You were beautiful even then.'

I took her arm and we left the smoky noisy room for the calm garden. There was a field behind the garden which looked every bit as tame and desiccated as the trim lawn and flower beds.

My brother and I were brought up in a bigger house, the one that burnt down, a little way away. It had the same over-clean smell to it and the same flattened garden. Even Hope Villa's small patch of grass with its low wall had more wildness than the creations of my parents. They could turn the Sahara desert into a suburban garden given a few years.

We stood at the end of the garden looking over the fence at the field beyond.

'It's all so flat, isn't it?' said Tessa.

'Yup.'

'And even the field smells of Sunday lunch.'

'You're right, it does.' I turned my back on the field and stretched my arms with an enormous yawn. I could see the party through the picture window. It was like being at an aquarium. All those mouths gasping out conversation and gasping in alcohol.

'This is power, is it?'

'It is part of the journey towards power. We're in the shallows now. This is the ordinary bit, the talking and the watching and the parties in suburban places, the being nice to dull people and noticing who else is on the journey, who else is watching and noting and calculating. We're at the early stage, remember. It gets more entertaining later on – the manipulation of politicians, the manipulation of wars, the arrangement of conferences and scandals.'

My brother and his wife were in the kitchen squabbling as we passed through. Usually they quarrelled because Annabel had been talking too intently or standing too close to some man. Sometimes they quarrelled because Annabel had admitted having an affair or indeed had been discovered doing so. She claimed she only did it to annoy Henry, because he was so horrible to her. In fact Annabel was the nearest to a nymphomaniac I have ever known. She flirted enthusiastically with me one Christmas afternoon when everyone else had gone for a walk. In this very house, in the spare room, we subsequently spent a very pleasurable if somewhat nerve-racking quarter of an hour. She is a pretty, blonde woman with an interest in horses and very little interest in her two small children who are looked after by a series of dissolute au pair girls. I have no idea whether or not Annabel informed Henry of our antics that Christmas day.

I thought that Henry probably put up with her affairs because they merely confirmed his own low opinion of himself and allowed him to hit her every now and again.

They appeared to be brewing up to violence. Tessa took one look at their cross faces and walked out of the kitchen, back to the room of men and women.

'How are things?' said Henry to me. He has short dark hair, longer legs than me, and a sneer in his eyes which make people distrust him at once. In spite of his vast capacity for work, Henry has not done especially well in his job as a lawyer because he is incapable of making himself pleasant to anyone for more than two minutes at a time.

'You're doing well, aren't you? You know our uncle is dying, or says he is. I think it's living alone in that house. And of course his sexual confusion. He doesn't know if he's gay or straight. He's always been right on the edge of things – never belonged, don't you think?'

'Oh – I've always liked him.'

I moved towards the door.

'That's because you think he might leave you his pictures,' said Henry with that disagreeable expression of his. 'Have you bothered to go to see him?'

'No, I haven't. He tried quite hard to belong, I think. All that money-making.'

'Always on the edge of things,' said Henry smugly again, obviously pleased to show himself capable of such talk. 'It must get very tiring. Don't you find?'

I smiled at him. 'Oh no. In my view, only the mediocre belong anywhere. They're in the middle you see, cosily in the middle. You were always in the middle at school – weren't you? But I'm sure that was nice for you.'

'I was not always in the middle,' he retorted, sticking out his lower lip childishly. 'I used to do very well in geography.'

I grinned.

'He's teasing you, Henry,' said Annabel. 'Try and behave like an adult for once. What's past is past.'

'What?' Henry puffed hopelessly, red in the face.

'Your mother was looking for you, Martin,' said Annabel with sweetly lowered eyes. 'Much to Henry's grief.'

'Ah well, no doubt we'll see you two again before we go,' I said, backing away. It was strange how many of their confrontations took place in the kitchen. Perhaps it was all those nice sharp knives and heavy saucepans which gave the rows an added piquancy.

In the main room faces were glowing with sweat and drink, and voices were raised with the desperation of a Sunday with a whole afternoon and awful evening before the blissful security of daily work resumed on Monday.

Tessa was presiding, a young Queen Elizabeth I, over her suitors. The disdain on her face seemed to enthral them far more than any traditional, welcoming, good looks could have done.

'Your Tessa's quite an asset,' whispered my mother to me. 'She has an extraordinary presence.'

She stepped in and took Tessa away from the smitten men to introduce her to John Bullard, a man with a comically large nose and horsey voice.

Mr Bullard's volume control went wild and made my mother and me jump. 'Your mother's marvellous,' he said.

When she wandered off he informed us that we could expect great things of her, which made her sound like a promising thirteen-year-old, not a fifty-four-year-old grandmother.

'I'm doing all I can to help her. All I can!'

'That's very good of you,' said Tessa.

'If there's any justice in the world,' he said in a low voice, 'your mother will be the next prime minister.'

I smiled.

'I'm serious,' he insisted.

After Tessa had concentrated on some skilful flattery of John Bullard, my mother bustled her on to the next victim.

'Would you mind,' she said in a soft voice, 'if I were to intro-duce you to a journalist from the *Observer*, Paul David? I'd so like him to feel he's had a nice time here. He's not been much of an... ally... up to now.'

'Of course,' said Tessa.

Shortly afterwards the balding man remarked to his friend, 'I see Paul David's taken with Tessa. He has that expression of amazement on his face as though someone's standing hard on his toe. I've seen that look before – it's Paul looking lustful.'

Tessa continued to charm a little feverishly each man she was introduced to.

She laughed, that pearly laughter, until it filled the room. It always arrived so unexpectedly and sounded so fresh and light-hearted, whereas everything else about Tessa was corrupt. Everything signified it; even her way of standing, very straight and tall yet with her head tilted, questioning, as though she were questioning everything, as though she were jeering at everything, even the things people hold most sweet. It was odd how attractive men find it is to be challenged.

Their own corruption was something more ordinary, to do with too much drink, too many meals, too many affairs with too many women.

That night there was a desperation about Tessa's lovemaking, as though she wanted to be annihilated by it, to forget everything forever. I love the smell of her and I love to hear her moans and murmurings and whisperings, and I love the taste of her sweat and the touch of her. The thrashing of her body beneath mine brings me to a pitch of desire I have never known before. And when it suddenly all stops with a scream, as though she's been stabbed, and her frantic body dissolves, loses its desperation, becomes soft limbs, soft skin, soft smells, again, it is as though we have created something which will last forever.

TESSA ARMSTRONG

Monday 25 September

THE ORDINARINESS OF SO MUCH EVIL – THAT'S WHAT depresses me. It's not that I want to do good or be good. It's the shabbiness of the alternative. I bet Hitler was a shabby little man, and Mrs Sherman, there's something very, very dull about her.

I know I'm not like that. I know there is something stronger and more defiant about my particular brand of evil, or whatever it is that makes me want to be the object of men's passions, to be the whore in the Reeperbahn window, the madonna in the alcove, that makes me want to twist and turn, to change myself into whatever they wish, to burn cities and have eyes burn with love for me.

But will I be dragged down into something sly, shifty, cunning, setting men against each other, making women hate me? I don't mind being hated, it's the pettiness of the hatred that I dislike. It's the thought of the woman staring into the mirror at her blemished skin and envying me the freshness of mine. It's the thought of men holding my image in their minds as they thrust themselves into the bodies of their bored wives. It's the ordinariness of every death Martin and I might inspire... that last gasp, the dribble, the shaking body.

Goodness, the goodness of my father for instance, is much more extraordinary.

I know I should cling to myself, whatever that is. Myself is all that I can be certain of. It's the nearest thing I have to a soul.

MARTIN SHERMAN

Tuesday 26 September

MRS MONSON, THE TWINS AND MR PHILLIPS ARE BEING very difficult about leaving Hope Villa. Really very difficult.

I called on the twins last night in their eyrie at the top of the house covered in posters about the bomb.

'It won't be long,' said Jerry.

'I know it won't be long,' said Mary.

'Nuclear war,' said Jerry. 'It's inevitable.'

'Inevitable,' echoed Mary.

They were sitting next to each other on the bed, very upright, fully dressed, skinny versions of Tweedledum and Tweedledee.

'Well,' I said, hovering at the door. 'You're supposed to have left here. I gave you money to go.'

'Go? We couldn't do that,' said Jerry.

'Couldn't do that,' echoed Mary.

'We have protest meetings...' said Jerry.

'Meetings...'

'Very important meetings.'

'About the bomb,' said Mary, gazing affectionately at her poster of a mushroom cloud as though at a photograph of some cataclysmic pop star.

'It won't be long, you see,' confirmed Jerry, smiling.

30

TESSA ARMSTRONG

Wednesday 27 September

IN THIS WORLD OF DISTANCES WE ARE VOICES ON THE TELE-phone, trying to link up. But what dangers there are. What inter-ruptions. What missed expressions. What pains can fill the space where the person should be, and what misunderstandings can be created by words without looks. Everything separate. The voice without the person. The words without the person to speak them. Everywhere there is distance, separation, confusion. Nothing links up. I can't make sense of it all. The thought of Martin makes me uneasy, as I sit alone in the room and feel the darkness inside me deepen.

Early on in his diary my father wrote:

It is odd that, although evil has claimed more victims in the past century than in any other, the devil himself should be seen as a figure of fun. Perhaps the devil is old hat, but that which he stands for should surely be respected and feared? Is it because churchmen appear on television and the devil doesn't that it is fashionable not to believe in him? But of course per-haps he does appear on television, in different forms, in soap operas, in newsreels, espousing different causes in different voices. The problem, as always, is in recognizing him. He has so many names.

31

MARTIN SHERMAN

Thursday 28 September

SHE'S GONE AND I DON'T KNOW WHERE SHE'S GONE. I suspect she's gone to see that Alexander Bartley. I wish I knew whether she loved him or hated him. I can't quite tell.

I never know quite what she's thinking. She's always a little withdrawn, as though dreaming of some other time, some other place, somebody else.

The room is desolate without her. This house is desolate too.

Upstairs I can hear the blare of the twins' music.

In the room next door I can hear Mr Phillips reading the Bible. He's walking up and down, reading, loudly:

'In the beginning God created the heaven and the earth.

'And the earth was without form, and void; and darkness was upon the face of the deep. And the Spirit of God moved upon the face of the waters.'

A small spider is running across my windowsill.

I wish Mr Phillips would be quiet. In his scarecrow clothes, and his gaunt yellow face, he looks like a prophet of doom. I can imagine him, up and down, up and down.

I wish Tessa would come back. The room smells of the scent she sprayed on her, and she has taken her red silk shirt and grey skirt from the wardrobe.

Yesterday I told her she hated Alexander Bartley.

'Oh do I?' she said, with that smile of hers. 'You should take care then. Hate and love are much the same. One can easily be exchanged for the other.'

'He killed your father. And now he's trying to become him. How can you put up with it?'

She shrugged. 'He's quite an entertaining person, quite charming, really.'

I wish Mr Phillips would be quiet.

'And God made two great lights…'

There is a smell of old stew permeating the house. Mrs Monson must be making one of her meals from cheap cuts of meat.

None of them should be in the house. They all said they would leave.

I can see a small cobweb up in the corner of the room.

The windows don't fit properly. It would be expensive to renovate this old dump. But it would catch alight very easily.

32

TESSA ARMSTRONG

Thursday 28 September

'SOMETIMES I GET WORRIED BY THE THINGS MARTIN SAYS...
and does,' I told Alexander.

We were sitting in the Club. I was aware of that odd light
in the back of his eyes which very attractive men often have, as
though someone were shining a spotlight through them.

'I'm not surprised. He's not exactly a pleasant young man.'

The light from his eyes was shining on me. I was in his spotlight, and he seemed in the dark, wide-eyed, watching me as if
watching a star he had waited all his life to see.

'Last time we met,' I said, with every effort to appear sincere,
'we couldn't really talk. We kept being interrupted.'

'That Nicola,' he said, 'I believe you were jealous of her.' He
tried to sit back a little, to be the relaxed, charming Alexander
Bartley, but he couldn't. He even attempted that chuckle of
his, the self-satisfied one: the raised shoulders, the smug closing
of the eyes. But it failed. He couldn't manage the carefree
twinkle of the eyes which was essential. The light in his eyes
was serious, spiritual. He was someone in a church, worship-
ping me.

'Oh yes,' I said, wide-eyed, 'of course I was. Had you ever...
had an affair with her?'

His mouth puckered up in delight.

'Just one night. I was a bit... drunk.'

'You're not really going to marry my mother, are you?'

'Is that why you phoned me?'

'Partly.'

'I am going to marry her. I can't have you so I'll have her. It's as simple as that.'

'You'll make her miserable.'

'How do you know that?'

'I know.'

'Not as miserable as she'd be without me.'

'She'd get over it. You see, now she thinks that if she married you, you'd be hers. But you won't be. You'll never belong to her.'

'And who do I belong to?'

I took a sip from the champagne glass, and then licked around my lips.

I looked around the room.

'They're watching you,' said Alexander. 'All around the room I can see men watching you. What is it about you? Your green eyes? Your grey hair? The way you hold your head? All this time, ever since that weekend in Belfast, I've wondered. Or is it perhaps just your sense of sin; that by making love to you again... if one were to make love to you... well, I'd feel I'd arrived somewhere I'd never been before, somewhere darker and more terrible and more beautiful. Do you understand?'

I watched a tall blond man pour his girlfriend a drink as he watched me.

'That sounds just like sexual desire,' I said.

'I've experienced sexual desire many times and it's not like this. Not what I feel for you.'

'Don't you desire me then?' I asked.

'Of course. I was... trying to explain.'

I laughed. 'It all sounds very difficult.'

'Even your laugh,' he said. 'It's very cold and hot at the same time. You seem to be made of opposites. Innocence and sin.

Conscience and amorality. Beauty... and something else, behind the beauty, which is hard to explain.'

'You're just saying I'm attractive, that's all,' I said.

'I wish that were so. But it's more than that. Sometimes... You know, I even wonder who you are.'

'This champagne,' I said, smiling at Alexander. 'I believe it's going straight to my head.'

He moved closer to me. 'I do... I do really love you,' he said.

'If you loved me, you wouldn't marry my mother.'

'It's you I want. I want you.'

He smiled at the pretty waitress who came by, and she flung him a backward look of flirtation.

He was relaxing now, losing that air of tension, of a man peering through windows, searching through photograph albums, feeling my clothes when the house was empty. The man who made the phone calls was changing into charming, adulterous Alexander Bartley.

'I hate this place,' I said. 'I don't know why we arranged to meet here.'

I saw a young girl with an old skin covered in wrinkles wave to a man over the far side of the room. It was as though someone had dragged their nails all over her face, over her forehead, around her eyes.

The woman she was with had skin made of leather.

Everyone in the room was chatting and laughing hectically. It was as though they were all convinced that if they stopped talking, if the music stopped, if they stopped waving and laughing, a great blackness would descend, and that would be that.

'What are they doing here, all these people?' I said.

'Nothing. Like the rest of us. They're just passing the time – making contacts, making love, filling in the hours.'

'This club reminds me of a film I saw once. Black-and-white. About a ship – a cruise. Everyone was having a great time. And then it gradually became clear that everyone on the cruise had died. *The Ship of Fools* I think it was called. The captain was the devil and all the waiters, all those severe gentlemen shaking up those cocktails with such expertise, were all his minions...'

Alexander lit up another cigarette.

'It's odd how nobody's noticing you today,' I said. 'Nobody's rushed over. They're not even looking at you. It's as though you don't exist.'

'They're looking at you. They can't see me.'

He tapped a long worm of ash into the ashtray.

'I feel quite peaceful,' he said. 'For the first time in a long time.'

His hair was pretty that night, washed and fluffy and fair as it had been when he came to collect me from my house all those years ago.

His skin was redder than it used to be, however, and there were broken veins around the nose.

'You know I don't really think I've been peaceful since you first smiled at me in that suburban garden, on that summer's day. I'd never have suspected that one smile could do so much damage to a man's life.'

'What smile?' I said. 'I don't remember a smile.'

As he talked about my smile, and about me, and about his love for me, I looked around the Club.

I enjoyed the effect I was having on the men in the bar, at the tables.

'After the accident my marriage quickly fell apart. I lost all interest in my wife the moment you smiled at me: that small double bed she and I had lain in the dark for all those hours together, those excellent dinner parties, the tasteful house with the stone-floored kitchen leading out into the garden, it all suddenly meant nothing to me. Even the children meant nothing to me.

'And I saw the world differently. Before I met you I never realized how ugly people are. You used to point out people in the street and re-dress them and re-organize their faces, with noses lower down the face or eyes further apart or lips thinner. For a few people you prescribed completely blank faces.

'You never seemed to be part of the world. You found even sensible things absurd, things like washing hanging on lines, or fences round gardens, or someone redecorating their house.'

'Compared to you, my wife was nothing, a mere squiggle on the face of the earth. I couldn't be bothered with her.'

Every now and again I would push my hair from my face to express vulnerability.

I ran my tongue over my lips.

I smiled to myself, as though in some private world of lust and secrets.

I knew the men in the Club would take my memory home and do things to that memory in their dreams.

I saw a bloated man with amusing eyes half listening to a beautiful blonde girl and half watching me.

And so they go on, all these people in clubs, people like the bloated man, and like Alexander, making love to people they don't love, and dreaming of those they do, or might, those they have never met, don't want to meet, will never meet. Dreaming and hoping that next time she'll be there, he'll be there, the person they've been looking for all their lives, through many lives, and have always just missed. She caught the bus just before their one – she had just left the party – she didn't turn up at that conference – she took another boat to another country. She's at work. She's the daughter. She must be avoided. Always a little distance away, just around a corner that is never quite turned in time.

And so they continue – all these men, all those women – stumbling around in the dark, in blindfolds, looking for what they never find, grabbing at dreams, in the end making do with something.

'He's the one man in the world for me.'

'He's the love of my life.'

I used to think that finding the love of your life was a kind of game. Each person was part of a pair but God or the devil had scrambled us all up, and the game of life was to find that person, to make a pair, like a grotesque card game. Spinsters and single men were those who had never been in the right place at the right time, and those who had married the wrong person were those who had made a simple mistake, said 'Snap' too quickly.

What a game. What an amusing diversion for God or the devil.

As soon as I saw Martin I said 'Snap' I suppose. Love at first sight. Instant recognition. Ordinary things.

We can do anything, he said. Now we've found each other we can do anything. There's nothing we can't do.

I smile. I charm. He schemes. Men fall in love. Men do as I ask. The world is ruled by men, and I can rule any man.

His powerful mother could introduce us to anyone. Martin can say whatever words are appropriate. We could play games with the world, and if the world is all there is, all there ever has been, as my father suggests, we can be playing games with the universe.

When the game of 'Snap' bores the devil, we could invent new ones.

We could invent games with ice and fire.

We could take the world into the past or into the future. Up and down the Snakes and Ladders.

It wouldn't be difficult – just a matter of stepping out, on to the stage, and starting to organize the games.

Up goes the thumb, down goes the thumb, the gladiators live or die.

But do I want that?

'But then,' Alexander was saying, 'that day when I came into your office, I couldn't keep my two lives separate any more – my secret one of loving you and my other public one, the one I lived with your mother.'

'You shouldn't have called in that day, you know,' I said. 'It reminded us both of things that should have been forgotten.'

'I'm quite aware of that. But I'd been so good for so long. Everyone breaks down eventually... I remember I stood wavering at the entrance of that office of yours, knowing that I had already left my other life outside, behind the plate-glass door, out there in the street with the people in raincoats and frowns and briefcases and sensible umbrellas. As I stood there waiting for you to turn, it was being blown away like other autumn things that were finished with.

'You stiffened a little, as though sensing something unfamiliar in the room, and you stopped typing and looked over your shoulder.

'Huge eyes, contemptuous mouth – it all came spinning into my face like sand, blinding me for a moment.'

Alexander was still staring in front of him, with a somewhat tragic demeanour (the waitress had gone), in part playing the role of star-crossed lover, with carefully prepared speeches. I have seldom seen Alexander be genuine, be himself, perhaps because that self doesn't exist and what he was performing now was the closest he could get to it. Perhaps the core of him never really suffers or feels much, although the scores of players all around him – Alexander the lover, Alexander the tragic figure, Alexander the family man – suffer and stumble across the stage.

'You were even more beautiful, I remember thinking,' he continued. 'You had lost that air of indulgent sensuality and become more austere. I liked your grey hair. I still like it.

'And now I'm staying in your house, and the house smells of you, the cups taste of you, I keep seeing your reflection in the mirrors, in the window panes.'

At that moment, as if on cue from some invisible stage director, he turned towards me, and his face registered some kind of lovelorn but noble emotion, and then at once that disappeared and it swam with the terror of loving me.

'It's true, damn you,' he said. 'That's the awful thing, that's the unbearable thing. It's all bloody true.'

'Excuse me, darling,' I said, and touched his arm.

I rose up and walked away from the table, knowing he was watching me.

In the cloakroom mirror there was that other self, smiling at me, waiting for me, both regal and childish, every man's dream.

Dark eyes, blacky-green eyes which express what men love most of all – not sweetness, not trust, but blackness, the blackness that lies at the end of things and at the beginning.

I returned to the main Club room wearing fresh red lipstick.

Alexander was lounging back, attempting to look insouciant again, his fair hair ruffled, his corduroy suit well-fitting, his eyes blue and smiling – the old, confident self.

'Of course,' I said as I sat down, 'it would have been possible for you to have avoided my mother, and me. It wasn't strictly necessary to have an affair with her.'

'But I wanted to,' he explained. 'Besides, my marriage was over. I wanted to marry again, I suppose, and Marian was available.'

Alexander chuckled, raising his shoulders in a self-satisfied, conspiratorial manner. His sparkling eyes puckered up into an expression of low cunning and self-delight.

'Plus, she was crazy about me and still is…' He lounged back still further, and gazed dreamily back into the past. 'Women tend to be, you know. It's because I treat them with a certain chivalry. Do you know I've been banned from one restaurant because I used to pick a flower from the tub outside to present to whatever girl I was lunching with? The girls always adored it.'

'Then why didn't you leave my father's wife alone?' I asked. 'As you say, it isn't as though she were the only person available. You're very sought after.' I shifted a little so that we were very close. 'And you're still very attractive.'

'Still? I'm only a young man.' He gave a smirk. 'Well, to be honest, I've always thought Marian a good-looking woman. I felt comfortable with her. I've always admired her. She gave Tom such a sense of stability, I think.'

'Tom had a sense of stability. She didn't give it to him.'

'I always admired Tom – you know. Such a decent kind of man.'

Alexander swept his hand over his forehead as though sweeping back a mass of youthful curls. In fact his hair was thinning now.

His eyes swam as he looked at me.

'You should have kept away. I don't understand why you didn't keep away.'

'I loved you…'

'You've been having an affair with my mother.'

'You wouldn't see me. I could be near you through your mother. Sometimes, she looks like you. Her laugh, sometimes, is like yours. The shape of her legs… Besides, I suppose I half enjoyed…'

'The spying on me?' I asked, with a sweet smile.

'Well… yes. I suppose everything had been so dull before. The affairs had been amusing enough but it had all been so easy, and I had felt sort of empty. There was nothing substantial there. It was all just a matter of gestures to ward off the loneliness and the blackness. It was just a big stage show put on every day, from the moment we woke up until the moment we went to sleep, when the real life started, the blackness, sleep. My wife was always so cheerful, unnaturally cheerful. We smiled, and had dinner parties, and I had my affairs to keep me sane, and all was delightful. It was only when I was in bed with a new girlfriend, when we'd got our clothes off and began tearing at each other, that I was in contact with anything remotely real. But you were real, horribly real, perhaps a little too real. Maybe I didn't really want you. I wanted to avoid you but I couldn't do without you. I wanted to spy on you through keyholes, dream about you at night, pick up titbits

about you from your mother, advise her on how to treat you, what
clothes to buy you… sometimes phone you, listen to your voice.'

'Stop it,' I said.

'It's still love, Tessa,' he said.

'But you love my mother too.'

'In my way.'

'You imagine that if you marry her you'll become substantial,
do you? By magic you'll stop having those awful heart flutterings,
those headaches, the sense that you aren't properly rooted here?'

'What are you talking about?'

'You told me you had heart trouble.'

'A little. You know,' he continued, 'I keep a picture of you in
my wallet.' He took it out. 'Look.'

The girl in the photograph had a fresh green uniform with
panama hat, white socks and a sultry expression.

'You're even lovelier now,' he said. 'I remember your mother
telling me on the phone that you'd gone into virtual retreat since
your father's death. I remembered being pleased. I didn't want you
going out, meeting boys. I used to imagine you in your room, in
your bed, between four narrow walls, trapped, in prison, waiting
for me. It always surprised me no one noticed you at the restaurant
that time. They believed I was with a prostitute, whereas I knew
I'd been with the most beautiful girl in the world.'

'Do your children mind you remarrying?'

'They don't seem to.'

'Don't you miss them?'

'Not really. Not often. I'm not crazy about small children. Not
like your father. He loved babies, especially. He used to talk about
his love for babies but nobody laughed. Nobody laughed at what
he said. But people often laughed at what I said. And he'd say ridiculous things. I remember one word for word: "It is extraordinary
that Christianity, which has at its heart the image of a newborn
baby as a saviour, has not more respect for the babies born every

day who are also saviours, examples of the truth behind the myth, reassertions of innocence and hope in a world made stale by compromise and the half-truths of experience." Now – did you ever hear a more pompous statement? But nobody laughed. They took what he said seriously. He had a kind of presence – whereas I, I am always the charming clown.'

By now we were on our second bottle of champagne, and Alexander's face was more puffed up. He had too much flesh on his face, too much skin lying in thick rolls over his bones. The sharp eyes stared out, windows into the soul, a rather dull soul. Not really wicked. Not even very bad. Just the soul of an actor who acts and acts and acts a variety of parts to prevent anyone noticing the dullness behind the gestures.

In my mind I could see him, wearing one of those brown velvet suits he thought so dashing, pick a dark pink carnation from a flower tub and present it to some foolish girl.

I could see him sitting slumped in a taxi asking another girl which restaurant she wanted to go to. 'Anywhere in the entire world,' he was saying, with a flourish of the voice which contrasted with the slumped figure who resembled an oversize plastic angel.

I could see him laughing with some seedy friend about a recent seduction.

I could see him writing an article with the articles by other people on the subject all around him, and in his face was that sly expression.

'Alexander, darling, you really should try to pull yourself together,' I said, before I abandoned him, drunk, desirous and confused.

I kissed him goodbye though, passionately, on the lips.

33

MARTIN SHERMAN

Friday 29 September

'TESSA. WHERE'S TESSA?' SCREAMED MARIAN ARMSTRONG at me. 'She's not in the house, is she? She's not in the fire? I was just on the way home and I saw the fire.'

I shook my head, but I didn't take my eyes off the fire which was tearing through Hope Villa, cracking the glass, sending billows of black smoke out of the windows as though a dragon were let loose inside.

She grabbed my arm. 'Tell me.'

'I didn't think you cared much,' I said.

'Of course I care about her. She's my daughter.'

'She's not in there. She went out.'

'Are you sure?' she screeched.

'Of course I'm sure.'

Although I was standing well back, with the rest of the crowd, I could still feel the heat surging out of the flaming building.

It was a magnificent sight.

I had almost forgotten quite how grand a fire can be. The firemen were a nuisance, spraying water all over it, but fortunately they could do little about it. It was far too powerful for the little men in their shiny hats and galoshes.

The crowd kept getting bigger and bigger. Every now and again I would look from the fire to the faces of the crowd. How they loved it. How they all loved it, standing so still, staring up, some faces glowing from the heat and the light of the fire. People enjoy destruction. They long for it – fires, plagues, devastation.

Mrs Monson and Mr Phillips burst out of the door coughing. He held her arm. It was rather touching. These disasters are not without their tenderness. He was so big and scrawny, with his hair all over the place like an old brush. And she, with her apron on, looked small, fat, rather lovable. Into the ambulance they went, together. Holding on to each other. I expect they'd never even touched before.

As for the twins, up in their altar to nuclear war – I can see them in my mind, clinging to each other, as the nuclear holocaust swept through the room, burning their posters, melting their records, setting light to the bed where they spent so much of their time. They could probably have escaped if they'd wanted to. But they probably thought there was no point. Their hour had come at last. The holocaust.

And of course it might just have occurred to them that the fire was nothing more than a fire. How disappointing that would have been. To climb out of the window, or fight through smoke on the stairs, and emerge into an ordinary street with all those ordinary houses still standing in their terrace, one after the other. How much better to cling together, die together, dramatically.

I liked the smell of the fire. It reminded me of Tessa.

I was angry earlier when I found she had gone.

She might have warned me. She might have told me who she was seeing. She thinks about Alexander Bartley. I know she does.

I was very careful to make it all look like an electrical fault. Although I was angry, I took great care.

Mr Phillips, Mrs Monson and the twins, they should have gone when I asked them to go. Really, they were dishonest to say they'd go and then not go. They should have done as I asked.

I heard Marian Armstrong's voice cry out, 'Tessa! You're all right. Thank God.'

I turned. They were clasping each other. Marian Armstrong had tears of relief pouring down her face.

But Tessa quickly broke off and shouted: 'Martin!'

I smiled as I pushed my way towards her. There was panic in her eyes. She doesn't know how much she loves me. And the second she saw me all the panic went.

'Martin,' she said angrily, 'what happened?'

'An electrical fault they think. Isn't it terrible?' I turned back to look at it. I found it hard to keep my eyes off the smoky building. I wished the police would allow us closer. Barriers were keeping us away.

She grabbed my arm and whispered in my ear, 'What have you done?'

I looked at her, all innocence.

'Where have you been? I missed you. I was anxious.'

'Angry you mean. Is everyone all right?'

'The twins. Unfortunately they haven't got out yet.'

Tessa ran towards the house. Both Marian and I ran after her and I managed to grab her arm and take her aside. Her mother watched, opening and closing her hands, her beige raincoat open at the front.

'God Almighty, Martin. They were only children,' said Tessa.

'They behaved like children. They were in fact in their early twenties.'

'Mrs Monson?'

'She's gone off clutching onto the arm of Mr Phillips. They made really rather a charming couple. She's got a bit of money from the sale of the house. Maybe they'll set up home together.'

'You're a shit, Martin,' she said, trying to break my grasp.

'Shh, darling. Don't use such horrible language. You should be grateful to me. I saved your diaries from the fire. Your diaries, mine, and your father's. They're all in this suitcase. All of our diaries. Saved for you.'

'Give it to me.'

'OK, OK, don't get cross, darling… remember I saw your face when you thought I was in the fire. But then you have a very expressive face. Even now, with your lower lip sticking out so crossly, you look so beautiful to me, you know.'

She kicked me hard on the shin, and began to force her way towards the house, through the crowd with their upturned faces still gazing at the smoke. But the heat drove her back.

I followed her, out onto Highbury Fields.

'Where are you going, Tessa?' I said, holding on to her arm.

'I'm going away. To think things out.'

'It's beautiful though, the fire, isn't it? You have to admit it's beautiful.'

'Yes.'

'And the smell, that corrupt, sinful smell, you like that too, don't you?'

'Yes. I like that too.'

'Kiss me, Tessa.'

I placed the suitcase beside her on the grass. I put my lips on hers and began to burn.

When our mouths came apart for a moment I felt utterly desolate.

'I do really love you, Tessa.'

'I must think for a while, Martin.'

She picked up the suitcase and began to walk away. I wanted to follow her. But I wanted to watch the fire too.

I turned and walked back to what remained of Hope Villa, through the autumn leaves with their black veins sticking up as the rest rotted.

34

Tessa Armstrong

Sunday 1 October

For two days and two nights I have stayed alone in a hotel room reading all of the diaries from the suitcase; Martin's, my father's, even some of mine, trying to establish the truth and deciding whether or not to leave Martin, and what to do about Alexander.

I chose a cheap hotel just round the corner from Victoria station, and I booked in under Nicola's name, Nicola Ward.

My room has thin orange curtains and stained covers over the twin beds. From the window I can see a black fire escape and the windows of the next-door hotel, which are draped in greying net curtains.

The area is not derelict; just a little run down, somewhere nobody stays long.

On occasion I can see shapes dressing and undressing behind those greying net curtains.

Usually I lie on one of the beds to read. I have never read Martin's diaries before, though I have often been tempted. His writing, with a blue biro, is thin and spidery:

But then I had that dream. I dreamt I met the devil standing under a lamp post at night, in the rain. With raincoat collar turned up and trilby turned down, he looked like a crook from an old black-and-white movie. And yet, as is the way of dreams,

I knew who he really was without his having to admit it. But of course I have seen him before in different forms.

Later, he wrote:

If I married her, then I'd be certain of her. Then I might have her forever. You see, I want to possess her soul as well as her body.

I read over and over again his description of our time together in Brighton:

We kissed and I wanted that kiss to go on and on. I wanted that kiss to last forever. It seemed unbearable that it should end, that each act of love had to end, that we could only be fused for a few moments, that one day we would be separated by death.

Afterwards, I went to the mirror and wondered if I would ever see Martin again.

I read my descriptions of our love-making. My writing, in black ink, is long and graceful. The pen seems to glide easily over the pages. And my diary itself, made of blue leather, is lovely too. Maybe it should all have burnt in the fire. Then perhaps I could have forgotten Martin and his kisses.

Martin's diary is just a few old exercise books, probably pinched from school. There is something oddly childish about all these words scrawled over the yellowy pages. He was frightened before he met me. But now he's not frightened. I found myself liking that more boyish, more frightened Martin. Is that why he let me have the diaries?

And now I have been alone for a long time, and all that time I've been looking for her, and I am growing tired of being alone.

Sometimes it seems that I've spent not just this lifetime but other lifetimes searching for her, and once I find her I can be myself.

As for the diaries of my father, I'm surprised my mother didn't have the sense to destroy them. But then she's never had very much sense. If she had sense she wouldn't be having an affair with Alexander now. She certainly wouldn't be marrying him.

He'll take everything from her and give her nothing. Once he's discovered that marrying Marian won't turn him into Tom Armstrong, he'll give up the whole idea.

I almost wish she had destroyed his diaries. I would not have had to read the following passages, written in blue biro instead of his usual brown ink. At times the biro dug into the paper and tore through it slightly.

I walked in on them.

She was lying in his arms, in our bed.

As simple as that.

My best friend and my wife.

The room smelt of scent.

Her hair was loose over the pillow and her face was flushed with desire.

Her eyes were oddly innocent. That was the worst thing.

She was innocent because she loves him.

Alexander, however, could hardly stop himself from grinning in victory.

She had sprayed scent all over the room, and put flowers on the dressing table.

She blinked at me.

I still couldn't quite believe it. It all seemed so improbable and yet so obvious at the same time.

His hair was lank from sweat, from the exertion I suppose.

They didn't spring apart. They just stayed where they were, very comfortable, as though this were something both were familiar with. Perhaps they had imagined me entering many times. Perhaps both for different reasons had wanted me to come in and find them.

'I came back to collect some things,' I said. 'Some cuttings I had left behind.'

Their skins were both naked, both close to each other. I was the intruder in my own house.

'Supposing Tessa had come home?' I said.

Marian sat up, and the bedclothes slipped down and I saw her full, beautiful breasts.

Alexander was watching me intently.

'It's nothing serious,' he said. 'Just... we drank too much at lunch.'

'Get out of my house. Now,' I said.

I watched as he got up, out of bed.

The smell of the scent made me feel quite sick.

'Please, get out,' I said.

I suppose, even before I read it, the scene had already existed in my mind.

After all, I had heard the new coldness in my father's voice when he spoke to Alexander and I had seen the way my mother looked at Alexander. I had read my father's distressed ramblings which suggested he too guessed that there was a deeper betrayal going on. And I had felt the atmosphere in our house during the weeks before my father's death: a restless, sexual atmosphere.

I remember her lingering glance into the mirror, her slight pouting of the lips, a new smell about her, some kind of special scent. Mother and daughter, he made love to us both.

I stood by the window of the hotel room. I could see the shapes of a man and a woman kissing behind the dirty net curtains of the hotel opposite. The sky was darkening, and below people were hurrying home, their collars turned up, their shoulders down, fearing it might rain.

On the evening of my second day at the hotel, I made a phone call.

'Hello. Yes. It's me. I want you to come to me. I'm at the Regent Hotel in Victoria, room 26, under the name of Nicola Ward. Why? I don't want anyone to find me. Please come. Darling. I'm sorry I've been hiding away. Come quickly. Come now.'

Slowly, I unbuttoned my shirt and took it off. I drew the curtains. I took off my bra too.

I went over to the mirror and looked at myself, and smiled.

I ran my tongue over my lips.

Then I dressed again.

The three diaries were lying on the spare bed: my blue leather one, Martin's exercise books and my father's written on lined paper between thick boards. I would have thought that as a journalist he would have typed everything. But perhaps diaries are something different, part of a private world linked by the changing shapes of a person's handwriting over the weeks.

There was nothing else much in the room except the remains of a cheese and tomato sandwich I had eaten at lunchtime, and an evening paper.

I went into my small bathroom and put on scarlet lipstick. I let down my hair so that it flowed all over my shoulders like smoke.

I wrote these pages while I waited. Outside, it grew darker, and in the room next door the radio was playing louder and louder.

35

MARTIN SHERMAN

Sunday 1 October

I HAVE BEEN SEARCHING FOR HER FOR TWO DAYS NOW.

I seem to have visited every hotel in London.

I wish I could work out where she is. I should know her mind well enough to guess – it's just like mine.

36

TESSA ARMSTRONG

Monday 2 October

YESTERDAY, AN HOUR AFTER THE PHONE CALL, I WENT DOWN the stairs, to wait for him outside. I liked the idea of meeting him outside, like a prostitute. That would appeal to him, I was sure.

It was a close, thundery evening, one of those evenings when no one is quite comfortable. Someone stares out of a window, walks into another room, looks at the time and wonders how it can still be so early. People's skin doesn't quite seem to fit them. It's a little too tight or a little too loose. They wonder about the future and think about the past. The heart – it seems to be beating rather loudly and unevenly in the long silence. Their little aches and pains enter the head and won't go away. An awareness of the dimensions of the body increases the discomfort. Such a little body really, taking up such a small amount of space. Even the strongest, widest arms are small really, covered with flesh, full of bone.

I have always liked the area round Victoria station. When I was a child I used to take the Tube here from Wimbledon, alone of course (I'd tell my mother I was at a friend's, and she never bothered to check). In those days I liked to be alone.

I like Victoria's lack of identity. People come here on the way to somewhere else. It lacks any kind of warmth.

Even the shops have a temporary quality to them. I never expected my favourite shop, which sold second-hand clothes, still to be there on my next visit, but it always was, a place of silver sequinned tight dresses, feather boas, fake diamond earrings and nightdresses made of chaste cotton, or lace or satin. I would try on the clothes in front of the mirror in the changing room, separated from the eyes of others by just a fluttering orange curtain.

I like the shifty little bed and breakfast places too, dilapidated houses calling themselves hotels.

I have always been comfortable here, wandering through the streets, noting the shop selling 'rubber goods' and the occasional smart restaurant where office workers could spend their company's money.

Alexander's suit, I noted, was a little too tight. But his hair, I must say, I have always liked his hair… those curls. Fallen angel curls.

I wore a brown leather jacket over my dress.

My shoes were sandals, gold sandals.

I have small feet. I watched them walking over the grey pavement.

I looked up.

Alexander took my arm and we walked up the stairs of the small hotel into a reception area with a yellow carpet.

The light bulb was dim.

My arm was around his waist.

We climbed up and up the narrow stairs.

He was walking slowly, but after one flight of stairs he was already a little out of breath.

We climbed up six flights. The hotel was really just a tall, thin house with a number of rooms. It wasn't exactly dirty, but it wasn't clean, and it had dingy carpets.

I turned round.

I put my head to one side.

'Aren't you going to kiss me?'

He moved towards me in the half-darkness.

He held my body.

Our lips pressed together.

The kiss lasted a long time.

When I pushed him away he opened his eyes and saw the expression of desire on my face.

'Why did you want me to come here?' he asked. 'To a hotel. After what happened?'

'I don't know. Perhaps because sometimes it seems the only thing that ever has happened to me.'

He took off my jacket.

He was unbuttoning my dress. He began to kiss my small breasts.

He kissed my neck.

'I've waited so long,' he murmured, taking off his clothes urgently. 'Your neck... it's so long, so beautiful. A swan's neck.'

He pulled me back on to the twin bed nearest the window.

He kissed my tummy.

He ran his tongue over my breasts.

'So lovely,' he murmured, as though in pain.

I dragged my fingers through his hair.

'Fuck me,' I said. 'Now.'

His heart was still beating fast from climbing all those stairs.

'Kiss me. Then fuck me,' I said, pulling his head up to my lips which did want to kiss his. So warm, drowning in the warmth, as his tongue penetrated my mouth.

We should have opened a window to let out the stale smell of empty rooms.

His body was beside mine.

He has such lovely skin, much younger than his face.

'My darling,' he said as we rocked together, sticking together.

He still had a furtive, appalled expression on his face, like a man gazing into a shop full of pornography.

For him, I was every vice, every passion, everything he had ever wanted.

My nails dragged down his back, drawing blood.

The dust in this place was in my nostrils as we rocked faster and faster.

And all the time his face had that intent expression, occasionally wincing with pain as I dug into his flesh.

When he came he shouted so loudly I feared someone would hear.

Afterwards he said he had never known anything like that, not even with me in the past.

It took him down and down – every scratch, every moan, sent him swirling deeper and deeper, he said.

My tongue and mouth were even more accomplished than before, he told me.

He lay on the bed, slightly apart from me, and he told me he felt as though he had been in a fight and was bleeding to death.

'You know your skin is very cold, even though it's warm tonight.'

His hair was sticking to his forehead and his heart was beating unnaturally fast.

'But I remember your skin was always cold,' he said.

I began to stroke his thighs.

'Let's do it again, darling,' I whispered. 'Now, no more talking.'

'Wait just a moment,' he said. 'I'm not… as young… as I was.'

He smirked, as though he were just using the cliché as a joke. His eyes closed a little as he grinned, and lines ran out all over his face.

'Now, darling, please,' I said.

My tongue played with his nipples.

We made love again.

He said my hair smelt strange that evening, that it smelt of ashes.

'You're not tired, are you?' I said, and laughed, after he had finished.

My skin was glistening with sweat.

'A little.'

'But we've waited so long,' I said. 'You've been hanging round me for so long, watching me, fingering my clothes, dreaming about me.'

'I know. I know that. But I want you for always. Not just now. Why don't we get married?' he asked. 'Please.'

I smiled at him.

'You can't have me for always.'

He traced his hand over my cheek, as Martin used to do. It already seemed a long time since I had seen Martin.

I climbed off the bed, walked to the window, and stretched.

I picked up my silk dress, slipped it over my head and began to do up the buttons.

He was leaning on his elbow, looking at me.

'But darling... you can't go yet... we will meet – continue our love affair, won't we?' he said. 'I do... need you.'

He was hardly able to speak, his mouth was so full of lust.

'You're marrying my mother,' I said. 'And you betrayed my father.'

I put my bare feet into gold sandals.

He was sitting up, leaning towards me, like someone hungry for a meal.

I looked back at him with narrow eyes.

'Tell me, Alexander, just one thing. Did you intend to kill my father that night? I have thought about it... a great deal. I've been here reading the diaries, and remembering... I think you did.'

'Of course not...'

'I want you to tell me the truth.'

Alexander was staring up at the ceiling. There was sweat all over his face.

'When I hit him, I wanted him to die.'

I was half listening to the radio in the room next door, and aware too of the sounds of the cars outside. I felt curiously peaceful.

I closed my eyes and saw again the expression on Alexander's face as he hit my father, that expression of satisfaction.

I ran my tongue over my lips.

'You are so lovely,' he said.

He had that blurred, rapt expression on his face. He was resting back on his elbows.

'You hated him, didn't you?' I said.

I came over to Alexander.

'Yes. I hated him. Him and his endless, relentless decency.'

'But he never did you any harm.'

I slid beside him, and began to caress him.

Warm skin. Alexander has always had warm skin.

'He did. He harmed me all the time. He could write better, was liked better. He was content.'

He moaned as I caressed him but he didn't close his eyes. It was as though he didn't want to lose sight of me.

'Tessa,' he moaned.

'Once more,' I whispered.

'Look, darling, I...'

I hitched up my dress, mounted him and enjoyed the ride, riding off into the night. As we went on and on and on and on for a moment I lost the sense of who I was and what I was doing.

I was aware of certain things: the grey hairs on Alexander's chest, the intent expression on his face, the wide, almost frightened look in his eyes, and my sense of triumph.

As for the room, I liked it all. The tiny bathroom. The yellow bedspread strewn on the floor. The sheets wet with sweat and semen.

I even liked, and was aware of, the net curtains which hung somewhere to my right, and the reproduction of Constable's *Haywain* which decorated the wall above the bed.

Each element was part of a bigger picture.

His lips were dry.

For a moment, I was sorry for him. My face showed him only desire. I didn't want him to see the hate. He didn't quite deserve that. Perhaps he thought I loved him. Perhaps I did a little bit.

He betrayed my father. And he killed him.

His curls were moist with sweat and he was breathing heavily.

I thought Martin's love would make me forget.

I could remember the night my father died.

I could see the windows of that Belfast restaurant looking out on the shadowed city.

I could feel the restlessness.

I could hear my father's voice:

A tiny pinball in space – nothing at all, and yet maybe everything there is. That quick, slow, everlasting twist of DNA. Spirals of life leading everywhere, staircases to heaven and hell.

I should like to forget my father now.

'Faster, darling,' I said.

I remember the way my father cried out that night – the shock, the moral indignation – and I saw Alexander's expression of pleasure.

As Alexander gazed up at me there was something odd about his face, as if he knew what I was thinking.

'I'm sorry,' he said, 'about your father. He was a good man.'

'That's right.'

For the first time, I really wanted him.

'Darling,' I said, squeezing his arms tight.

Perhaps Alexander wants to be free too.

I can hear his heart beating so loudly it must deafen him.

But I can hear the thunder too, outside, as the rain slashes against the window.

The thunder brings a cool breeze from the shaking window frame.

And I can hear laughter too. From a next-door room perhaps.

There is so much sweat. I seem to be floundering in sweat.

He is clutching on to my red dress which swirls around us. I take it off.

I lean down.

'Love me,' I whisper. 'Come on, Alexander, love me.'

I slip down beside him and move him on top of me.

'Love me,' I say again.

The laughter in the room next door is getting louder. But Alexander doesn't appear to hear it. He is putting all his concentration on the movement of the body, on keeping himself going.

Am I enjoying it?

Sort of.

'I love you,' he said.

The room is really quite dark, except for the distant lightning which illumines it from time to time.

I have always been able to see well in the dark. Cat's eyes, my mother used to say.

'I love you,' he said again.

Every now and again Alexander's body squelches against mine and I try not to smile.

I don't want him to see that I am amused by this. He is so very serious and humourless this evening.

Isn't Alexander ever going to stop I wonder?

I look up again into his face and see that tenderness and almost regret… there is something so sweet about Alexander, always an adolescent, a naughty adolescent seducing as many girls as he can, and sucking out as much pleasure as possible from his life. He's been such a good actor, really, and played all kinds of roles, as long as they were starring ones.

'Tessa,' he cries out in pain.

'Darling,' I say, smiling.

MARTIN SHERMAN

Monday 2 October

I KEPT THINKING OVER EVERYTHING SHE HAS SAID TO TRY to work out where she could be, what she could be planning, if she could have booked in somewhere under another name. I phoned up Marian Armstrong, who claimed she had no idea where Alexander was. She wants to report Tessa to the police as a missing person.

But then I remembered something Tessa had once said to me about liking the area around Victoria station, because it is a place of intersections.

Tessa Armstrong

Monday 2 October

His body collapsed on me heavily and it was difficult to push off.

I could have sworn that his empty face was smiling, a little smugly.

Perhaps he was pleased to have died like this. 'She screwed me to death,' he would boast, in hell.

It was growing very dark.

But I wasn't afraid.

Even as he lay there, so little remaining of him, I felt a rush of high spirits. I could be myself again at last.

I piled my hair on to the top of my head, looked into the mirror and smiled. Grey, entangling hair, smelling of ashes.

I kissed him – and my lips were far colder than his.

It was the stillness of the room that was strangest of all, a pause before something else starts.

Even the radio in the room next door had stopped playing.

I was glad not to hear the thump of Alexander's heart any more.

I went to the window and looked out. All I could hear was some birds calling to each other against the murmur of traffic.

The couple behind the net curtains of the hotel opposite continued to caress.

In the window I could see the pale glow of Alexander's face on the bed behind me.

I opened the window and the air blew in, chasing out the stench of the past.

I ripped some pages from my father's diaries and tore them into small pieces, then threw handfuls out into the night sky.

They floated down, holy confetti I no longer needed or wanted.

As the pages tore I heard my father's voice:

Perhaps we are all there is. If that is so, every action each individual takes is a huge event, something of universal consequence.

Odd that I loved Tessa so much, that I love her so much. It's her spirit I love – the unconquerable human will.

Someone was knocking on the door but I just continued to tear.

'Let me in,' said Martin. 'Let me in.'

'I'm busy,' I called out.

'Let me in,' he said again in a loud whisper.

'Go away.'

'It's Martin. Darling. You must let me in.'

I stopped and went over to the chipped yellow door.

'I've missed you. Let me in, now.'

My hand reached out and turned the key in the lock.

He sprung forward to hug me.

I moved back.

He saw Alexander lying on the bed, and quickly closed the door.

'Tessa. What have you been doing?'

He looked round the wrecked room – the clothes strewn round, the bunched up bedclothes, the smell of sweat and desire.

'His heart,' I said. 'It failed him.'

'So I see.' Martin was watching me closely with increasing awe. 'I think… Miss Nicola Ward… it would be better if you left now. No wonder you booked in under another name. I've been round every hotel in Victoria. Nicola Ward will have some explaining to do… is it too late to phone an ambulance?'

'Far too late,' I said.

'Your mother will be heartbroken.'

'It'll be the best thing for her. He was unfaithful. He didn't care for her.'

'Tell me, how many times did you make the poor man make love to you?'

'Four, about,' I said.

Grinning, Martin put out his arm to me, and the words from his diaries came into my head.

I have seen him as the charming Mephistopheles of *Faustus*.
I have seen him swinging his umbrella in inventive old films.
I have seen him by my bed at night as a child. I have seen in the mirror.

'So you've come for me, have you?' I said.

He nodded.

I stared at Martin, not knowing quite what to do, quite what to say.

After what seemed a long, long time, I laughed.

'I think I'd better get dressed first, don't you?'

Also by Sally Emerson...

Heat

'A story of obsession and love and the difference between the two...
Emerson writes superbly about the dark side of love'

Sunday Times

'Quivering with subtle erotic tension and sparkling with observation... a hypnotically menacing, emotional thriller'

Mail on Sunday

'An enticing novel made chilling by the juxtaposition of happy
family life and undefined terrors'

Sunday Express

'Sally Emerson has done something remarkable: in *Heat* she has
restored passion to the serious English novel... and takes it and its
companion obsession as seriously as Emily Brontë did. Yet that is
what Sally Emerson has dared to do, to remove *Wuthering Heights*
from the Yorkshire moors and place it in a long, hot Washington
summer'

Allan Massie, *Scotsman*

'Brilliant... economy and style'

Sunday Telegraph

'A thriller of Hitchcockian dimensions... Permeated with eroticism
and danger... A really gripping book that captures perfectly the
seesawing state of mind of its heroine'

Daily Telegraph

Separation

'A triumph… dark and scary and humorous and oddly moving'

Literary Review

'Emerson is a writer who excels in portraying the darkness beneath polished surfaces… the real heart of the novel is the inexplicable power of children over their parents… calculated to unleash strong feelings in the least maternal of readers'

TLS

'Set against a wittily evoked background of the confident professional classes this frequently moving and accomplished novel deserves to be widely read'

Times

'Sally Emerson's assault on marriage is as lively as her panegyric on babyhood. For sensitivity hitched to wit, she is a delight to read'

Mail on Sunday

'Thoroughly gripping… poignant, absorbing and terribly heart-rending'

Scotsman

'Tight and controlled… Emerson's skill is to subvert the humdrum with sinister undercurrents'

Sunday Times

Second Sight

'Sally Emerson excels in razor sharp observations'

Times

'*Second Sight* is a very clever first novel about youth and its careful obsessions, and middle age and its careless sexuality... It has more than a little of Iris Murdoch's style, wit and sense of the bizarre'

Cosmopolitan

'*Second Sight* is a remarkably well-managed story... there are brilliant chapters on the murder case... Sally Emerson is a highly original, creative novelist'

Eric Hiscock

'Strong, individual and full of promise'

Financial Times

'Ambitious and intriguing'

London Evening Standard

Listeners

'Sally Emerson is a novelist of unusual penetration and sureness of touch'

'The author is one of the brighter luminaries on the literary scene… she has the gift of making human eccentricity look and sound down to earth and her dialogue is unerringly sharp'

'Crisp and entertaining… Read on'

'Sally Emerson writes simply but selectively. She plots and times her revelation of character or event with such precision that the reader is drawn deep into the ramifications of her heroine's panic'

Broken Bodies

'This is a most remarkable and elegant novel: steely too, swishing this way and that like a fine blade, catching present and past with a kind of icy dexterity. It has echoes of early Murdoch, at her most crystalline, or Durrell without the ornateness. It is also, of course, intensely romantic'

Times

'Sally Emerson has an enormous gift for holding the reader in a close and forceful grip'

New Statesman

'A serious class act. This is a wonderful book. Sally Emerson's writing is elegant and controlled and her observation of detail – the superfluous sounds you listen to when someone else is speaking, for example – is marvellous... The ending is wonderful, unexpected, and perfect. I wish I could tell you what it is'

Sunday Express

'There are times, often, when Sally Emerson, in the suddenness of her prose and smooth abruptness with which she changes key, recalls Muriel Spark. She has something, too, of Spark's uncanny ability to suggest the fragility of our civilized state, the menace that lies just below the surface... read it quickly; savour it at your leisure'

Allan Massie, *Scotsman*